Personal Solicitor

Michael Pickford

Personal Solicitor is a work of fiction. Names, characters, places, and incidents are either a product of the author's imagination or are used fictitiously. Any resemblance to actual persons, deceased or alive, events, or locales is entirely coincidental.

ISBN:9781521218273

DEDICATION

To my loving and patient wife!

and

To You – The Reader.

Thank You!

ACKNOWLEDGMENTS

Thanks to my wonderful wife for the hours she spent using her expertise to edit this book. She's a stickler. You can enjoy a clean, crisp book because of her tireless work. If you encounter any grammatical problems, it's my fault for not catching all of the corrections she suggested.

ONE

THE CLOCK ON THE wall above the coffee cabinet said 7:35. It was Tuesday morning. Tyler Kane finished his morning run on the local Greenway, cleaned up, and drove to his office at 124 Front Street in Smyrna, Tennessee. He made some coffee and sat at his desk to browse through the local newspaper.

Kane, as everyone called him, was forty-two years old. He was in excellent physical condition and was careful to stay that way. High cholesterol, high blood pressure, and high blood sugar didn't just run in his family they galloped. All of his numbers remained better than textbook because he worked hard to stay fit. At six foot three inches tall, he had a lean body, broad shoulders, and a mild manner. His presence was one of silent strength. The gleam in his dark hazel eyes reflected his keen mind and quick wit.

Kane's offices were modest but modern. The

front office had a secretary's desk, a fax machine, and a couple of rarely used chairs for clients to sit in while they waited to see Kane. A Persian rug woven with a modern, unobtrusive pattern covered the center of the hardwood-floored room. A simple lamp and a couple of coasters sat on a small round table between the two sitting chairs. A few "Old South" paintings hung on the walls. A door behind the secretary's desk led into Kane's office.

Kane sipped his coffee and browsed the political column when he heard a buzzer ring. Someone entered the main door out front. He heard a knock on his office door before he could get out of his chair. The door opened quickly, and the young, fresh face of Leann Walker peeked in and said,

"Good morning, Mr. Kane. You have a visitor, a young man."

Kane was perplexed. He thought for a moment about what to say. He finally asked, "What's his name?"

"He says his name is Jeremy. He has a problem he wants to discuss with you."

"Don't you believe his name really is Jeremy?"

"Why yes, I mean, I have no reason to think otherwise."

"Did he show you some identification?"

"No, he didn't. Should I ask for some?"

"No, please don't," Kane said. "Did he discuss the nature of his problem with you or give you any details?"

"No, he said it was something he needed to discuss with you."

"That's good. What's his manner?"

Leann looked confused, "His manner?"

Kane sighed, "How's he acting?"

"Oh, he seems nervous and somewhat guarded. I'd say he was downright frightened."

"About how old would you say he is?"

"He couldn't be much more than high school age, maybe in his first or second year of college."

Kane's voice was deep but not overbearing. It was resonant, clear, and smooth. He rarely spoke with excited tones. He had the kind of voice that got one's attention and held one's interest without the need for the flare of exaggerated intonation. He usually reflected a serious manner when he spoke.

"Very well," he said to the young lady. "I'll see him in a few moments. There's a pressing matter I need to discuss with you first."

"Of course, Mr. Kane. What would you like to discuss?"

"Well, for starters," Kane said, "who are you, and why are you running around my office playing the role of secretary?"

TWO

IT WAS A BEAUTIFUL spring morning in Middle Tennessee. It was earlier that same Tuesday morning, and the local weatherman with his usual cheerfulness promised a warm sunny day with a light, comfortable breeze. He spoke with the confidence of someone who thought they manufactured the weather personally.

Linda Richard's alarm went off at five thirty a.m. sharp—her normal time. She changed into her walking gear and headed out for her morning walk. Her routine was well-known throughout the neighborhood because she'd followed the same pattern for many years.

Linda was fifty-five years old, but she looked and felt like a woman in her late thirties. She was serious about her exercise and healthy eating habits.

Linda exited the large house through the back door off the dining area and onto the back deck. She walked around the swimming pool, down some wooden steps off the side of the deck, through a gate, and onto a walking path. The path led down to the main road.

The Richards lived on Heavenly Way, a winding country road on the outskirts of Smyrna in the wooded Rock Springs area. They built their house ten years earlier, just before the recession began. The house boasted forty-two hundred square feet of old-style decorum mingled with modern architecture. It was a comfortable place to live and provided a pleasant and interesting site for passersby to view.

Developers had planned other houses for the fairly new Heavenly Way, but the recession put a stop to them. There were only two other houses on the street. Both were built in the same year and by the same builders as the Richards' house. But the three houses weren't constructed according to a cookie-cutter pattern. The builders designed and constructed each house with unique characteristics. They complimented the other houses, yet they had their own distinct charm.

One of the houses lay south of the Richards' house about two hundred and twenty yards away. The other house was a quarter-of-a-mile north of the Richards' house near the main entrance of the street. Linda and her husband enjoyed close friendships with the families who lived in both the other houses. They slept better at night knowing their neighbors were also trusted friends.

Linda stepped off the pathway onto Heavenly Way and picked up her pace. She tried jogging years earlier and decided it wasn't for her. But she stuck to walking and thoroughly enjoyed it. She added a daily swim to her routine during the warmer months of the year.

Linda usually thought through the activities she'd planned for the day while she walked. Her regular course was to walk up to Rock Springs Road, turn around, and walk back to the end of Heavenly Way. Then she'd walk back up to Rock Springs Road then back to the house for her morning swim.

She noticed how all the trees had clothed themselves so quickly that year. She walked toward Rock Springs Road and saw faded buttercups just beyond the ditch to her right on the same side of the road as their house. A variety of fresh, colorful spring wildflowers sprang up to replace them. A thick wall of trees freshly dense by the new late-spring foliage lay behind the flowers and other brush. A large open field sat behind the trees, but it was impossible to see because of the dense trees and brush. The field lay just north of the Richards' house—it would be to one's left as they faced the house from the street.

Linda heard a sound in the distance beyond the trees. It resembled the sound of metal hitting metal—a muffled clanging sound. It startled her for a moment, but she kept up her pace. She felt comfortable walking their street in the early mornings. The area proved to be safe and exempt from any remnants of the violence and gang-related activity just a few miles up the interstate toward Nashville. She was proud of their capital city for the way they controlled and suppressed the gangs so efficiently.

She got closer to Rock Springs Road. Her heart rate increased. She felt the familiar burst of energy brisk exercise produces. That's when she usually focused her mind on the activities of the day. But her thoughts drifted toward her husband.

She left her husband in bed asleep—as usual. He liked to read late in his study and wake up around six thirty in the morning. He'd shower, eat, have coffee, and leave for his office in the Southeast part of Nashville. His routine was as reliable and predictable as hers. He'd usually be gone before she finished her morning swim.

Something was nagging at Linda's mind lately about her husband, Don. He'd been preoccupied and slightly distant the previous few weeks. He hadn't said or done anything shocking or out of the ordinary, but a wife could sense when her husband was troubled by something. Don was always careful not to bother her with his affairs. He hadn't said anything about any problems he might be dealing with.

"Don is a good man and a considerate husband," Linda reminded herself.

Don took care of all the finances in the family. He worked hard and made good money. He balanced the accounts, paid the bills, handled the investments, monitored their savings, and kept up with the insurance premiums. All she had was a credit card to buy whatever she needed whenever she needed it. She never heard a single complaint from him. But lately, something wasn't right.

"Oh well, it's probably nothing," Linda thought

to herself. She finished her walk and stepped onto the pathway. She walked around the house to the steps attached to the deck. She stepped into the changing room at the back of the deck, changed into her swimming gear, and dove into the pool.

Linda was a tomboy growing up. She grew up in the country around creeks, ponds, and lakes. She learned to swim at a young age and could easily out-swim the most competent fish in the waters. She glided easily across the swimming pool. She swam to one side of the pool, turned quickly and lithely, kicked off the side, and swam swiftly to the other side. She swam fifty laps.

She finished her last lap, got out of the pool, dried off, and went to the back of the deck. Her husband paid to have an outdoor shower stall installed a couple of years earlier. Linda balked at the idea at first because of her deep sense of modesty, but Don considered that when he had it constructed. She loved the way it turned out.

The stall was made up of four simple well-frosted glass panels, a seven-inch overhead rain shower faucet, and beautiful floor tiling. A fully tiled wooden-sided stall connected to the side of the shower stall. Linda stepped into that stall, dried off, and put on her robe. She stepped back into the shower area and stepped out through its door onto the deck.

Linda felt refreshed and fully charged to face the challenges of the day. Then she felt a slight tickling sensation in the upper-middle part of her back just between her shoulder blades. A mild burning sensation followed. An instant later, her vision faded and she lost consciousness.

It was a beautiful spring morning showered with the songs of native birds newly returned from their migration. Freshness and vitality filled the air—Mrs. Linda Richards' body lay lifeless on the hard, wooden deck.

THREE

JEREMY SCOTT CLOCKED OUT at exactly six thirty on Tuesday morning. He worked at a local donut shop in Smyrna called Devilish Dunkers every Monday through Friday. He clocked in every morning at three a.m. and clocked out at six thirty a.m. without variation. The store opened at six. He spent three hours baking donuts and cleaning up in the back. Then he kept an eye on the front counter until the regular cashier began her shift at six thirty.

He almost didn't get clocked out on time that morning because a local customer started up a casual conversation with him about celebrities who lived in the area. The man mentioned two or three country music stars. Then he seemed especially keen on a local legal star who inadvertently gained a moderate amount of fame because fans generated some websites that cataloged and dramatized his more notable accomplishments. The man even gave Jeremy one of the lawyer's business cards.

Jeremy listened politely but with little interest. He casually took the card, slid it into his pocket, thanked the man for coming in, and bid him a good day. Then he walked swiftly to the time-clock and clocked out.

Jeremy enjoyed the sunrise during his drive home at certain times of the year. But the sun had risen at 5:01 a.m. on that particular morning, normal for late May. The early morning scenery was still beautiful even though he missed the sunrise.

While he drove home, Jeremy almost forgot he wasn't going home. Some of his neighbors asked him to stay in their house and house-sit while they were away for a couple of weeks. The Hensleys were good neighbors and close lifelong friends with Jeremy and his parents.

Jeremy arrived at the Hensley's house at six forty-five a.m., precisely the time he'd arrived the previous morning, and just about the same time he arrived at his own house just up the street when he went home. Jeremy entered the house, put a bagel in the toaster, and ran upstairs to the room where he was staying. He wanted to take a shower. He was anxious to get the smell of donuts off of him. He loved donuts, but the smell reminded him of work. Besides, he'd recently changed his diet and began jogging around the neighborhood in the early evenings. He took up jogging to get healthier, but the routine also served as a pleasant break from the monotony of his daily studies.

Jeremy was getting dressed after his shower when he heard a strange sound. It came from the end of the hall. He walked into the hallway to investigate. The sound got louder as he eased toward the bedroom at the end of the hall—it sounded like an alarm clock.

"Why is there an alarm clock going off?" Jeremy thought to himself.

He walked down the hallway and determined that the alarm was coming from the Hensley's bedroom. He didn't feel comfortable going into their private bedroom, but he couldn't very well allow that alarm to go off for another twelve days.

Jeremy opened the bedroom door slowly and carefully as if he expected to find the Hensleys sound asleep in their bed. He chuckled to himself for being so ridiculous. He entered the large, comfortably arranged bedroom, found the light switch, turned on the light, and oriented himself with the layout of the room. The alarm was coming from the clock on the side of the bed nearest the door. He walked over to turn it off.

He reached for the clock and stopped dead in his tracts. Something startled him—cold chills went up his spine. A strange object lay on the nightstand just in front of the digital clock. Jeremy overcame his initial bewilderment, picked up the object, and investigated it further.

His widened eyes passed over the contents. His mouth cocked into a half-open position. His neck bent slightly and pushed his head closer to the object. Slowly and quietly, he mouthed the words, "What in the world…?"

FOUR

TYLER KANE SPOKE WELL but listened even better. He was patient when someone was speaking to him and resisted the urge to interrupt with questions and observations. His keen analytical mind allowed him to visually outline everything he heard in a given conversation while he simultaneously formulated the proper responses to give and questions to ask when the one speaking to him finished.

Leann Walker parked herself gracefully, yet professionally, in the chair opposite Kane's desk. She explained to him with a disciplined, bubbling excitement how she came to be in his office.

Kane sat upright in his chair, leaned slightly forward, rested his arms on his desk, and listened intently and stoically to all she had to say. He occasionally nodded or sipped his coffee as he listened.

"Why you're Mr. Tyler Kane, of course. Tyler

Kane, PS to be exact, as your shingle out front indicates. The PS, of course, stands for 'Problem Solver.' You've traveled extensively with your business, but you were born and raised right here in Rutherford County. You've lived here all your life. You attended law school in Texas and graduated at the top of your class. Then you became your grandfather's protégé. He taught you all the ins and outs of corporate law with an emphasis on negotiating.

"After your grandfather passed away, you put together a team of five specialists and became an Independent Negotiator, a highly successful one at that! You were married but had no children. Your wife passed away in a tragic car accident when you were thirty-eight years old.

"You enjoyed years of overwhelming success in your corporate law business, but you retired just after your wife passed. You took off a full year to mourn and recuperate. After that, you hung your shingle here and opened up this office with the unique title of 'Problem Solver.'

You've successfully helped all your clients overcome their problems over the past three years. Not all those problems involved the law, but, when they did, you invariably left a capable local DA's office dumbfounded, bewildered, and defeated!"

Kane considered Leann for a moment when she finished speaking. His stolid deep stare made her feel a bit nervous and uncomfortable. He lifted his chin and spoke in an even tone.

"Well," he said. "How do you know these things about me? I certainly don't go to any trouble advertising myself."

"The internet, of course," Leann said. "You're very popular, Mr. Kane. Did you know there's even a page dedicated to you on social media? It has thousands of followers. A handful of people run dedicated blogs about you too. Those are popular as well."

Kane shook his head, "Of course, the World Wide Web."

Kane wasn't a wild fan or avid user of the internet. Not for personal interests anyway. He was old-fashioned when it came to things like "shopping and browsing." He preferred to walk into a department store and find the items he wanted. If they were articles of clothing, he tried them on, paid for them, and walked out with those items in his hands.

He also preferred the telephone and "real-time" visits when he communicated with family and friends. He felt the internet, especially social websites and apps, allowed too many people to know too many details about the people they "friended." He was also concerned about the growing threat of strangers who accessed web users' information through shady means. He used the internet occasionally in his professional life though.

Kane made a note to himself while Leann talked. He decided to contact those who ran the websites and have the web pages removed. He wasn't angry at them. In fact, most people would be flattered by the attention and the "fame." Fame, however, didn't interest Kane. He felt those internet pages could lead to some uncomfortable and potentially dangerous situations for both himself and others in his life.

Kane looked intently at Leann Walker and said, "Young lady, you've summarized my life and my business fairly adequately. Though, I dare say some of it was exaggerated and romanticized. But you've failed to address my original question. Who are you, why are you here, and why are you running around my office playing secretary?"

"Well, my name is Leann Walker. I'm twenty-five years old and single. I was born and raised in Murfreesboro, graduated high school with a 4.0-grade point average, and attended law school in Nashville. I passed the lawyer license examination with flying colors. I haven't taken the Bar examination yet, but I intend to soon. I aspired to be a prosecutor but recently decided to go into criminal defense instead. I'm also an avid—"

"Never mind, Miss Walker," Kane inserted, "We'll talk more about it later. Right now, we need to attend to our nervous guest. Now, I'm assuming you're interested in working with me. Or are you here merely as a curious, star-struck stalker?"

Leann's eyes sparkled at the comment. The corners of her mouth creased into a playful smile. She said in a mock "valley-girl" accent, "Why, as a curious, misguided stalker, of course."

Kane was a fairly good judge of people. He made mistakes on occasion though. He decided to trust Leann Walker to a certain extent based on what he'd observed about her so far. She was young, intuitive, capable, and had a zeal for life.

She also seemed to have a keen interest in mystery and adventure. She was obviously a fan of him or at least of the man those web pages portrayed. That meant she had the necessary traits for professional devotion—something he required in an assistant. She was a little misguided in her endeavors, and was misinformed about some of his life's details, but she could well become just what he needed in a secretary and assistant with some work.

She was attractive and presentable. Her attire was modest yet modern. She was smart and quick-minded. She also spoke clearly and succinctly—but a bit excitedly.

Kane desperately needed to replace his former secretary. He depended on her heavily. She'd recently reunited with an old flame online, married, and moved to Chicago. He wondered if she had internet fans too.

Kane wasn't a lazy man when it came to taking care of business at hand. But he liked for all the particular and routine things in his life to be in place. He didn't like spending the time and energy necessary to put them back in order when they became disheveled. So, he'd taken no steps to find a replacement for his former secretary although she left nearly three weeks earlier.

Leann Walker just saved him the trouble of advertising for a new secretary not to mention conducting mundane interviews. He did need to know more about her, but that could wait. He had a potential client who needed his assistance. Tyler Kane was fully devoted to those who had the good fortune of becoming one of his clients.

"Okay," Kane said, "I've got a few papers you need to sign before we speak with Jeremy. This is on a trial basis you understand. These papers will give you temporary employment at this firm. You'll be my official assistant. That will bring you under lawyer-client privilege protection. I'll need you to be fully involved should this problem of Jeremy's lead to him becoming a client and to possible subsequent court proceedings. Is that acceptable?"

"Why, yes, Mr. Kane, absolutely. Thank you! You won't regret this. I won't let you down—"

Kane interrupted, "And one other thing. When we're in official settings I like to keep things official. You'll call me Mr. Kane and I'll refer to you as Miss Walker. But around the office and in other casual settings, I'll call you Leann, and you can call me Kane."

Leann nodded her approval.

Tyler Kane, PS would soon learn two things. First, Leann Walker, although highly educated, was still naïve and uninformed about several things. But she was very knowledgeable and efficient in matters that would benefit him in his work. Second, the peculiar circumstances surrounding the young man who called himself "Jeremy" wouldn't only interest Kane, but they'd present him with his greatest legal challenge yet.

FIVE

KANE'S OFFICE WAS MODEST and comfortable. The people who wanted his services were troubled about the matters they wanted him to address. He believed that a warm, inviting environment helped put them at ease. He wanted to make it easier for them to get to the heart of the matter when it came to gathering the necessary and essential details of their concerns.

There was a large window on the back wall behind Kane's dark leather desk chair. The desk was solid and made of dark, rich-looking cherry wood. The back panel of the desk facing the guest chairs was plain and smooth. There were no designs or wood carvings of any sort. Kane believed those things would distract his clients as they relayed their story and answered his questions.

The left wall was covered from floor to ceiling with plain bookshelves made of the same dark wood as the desk. Those shelves were filled with law books neatly arranged. The wall opposite that wall had identical bookshelves. Pleasure-reading books and a handful of tastefully framed personal photos were on its shelves. Most of its shelves were empty, but they didn't look barren because of the intentional arrangement of the items that were on them.

A cabinet/shelf combo sat against the front wall next to the door. It housed a coffee maker, cream, sugar, and other items to facilitate the making and consuming of the dark brew that Kane cherished. A small refrigerator sat there as well. It all looked neat, professional, and lavish in a simple way.

Plain, dark burgundy cloth covered the two padded guest chairs. The wooden armrests, frame, and legs of the chairs were the same dark wood as the other pieces of furniture in the room.

A high-quality thin-pile rug covered the hardwood floor. It matched the cloth on the chairs and the curtains. A small table made of cherry wood sat between the guest chairs. On the table were two coasters, a leather writing pad, a couple of pens, and a small box of tissue.

If you walked into Kane's office, a sense of order, professionalism, and warmth would greet you—embellished by the comforting aroma of freshly brewed coffee.

Kane, Leann, and Jeremy sat in their respective chairs in Kane's office. Kane had asked Leann to go out into the front room to get Jeremy. She found him pacing the room from one wall to the other. Leann didn't know it yet, but that was why the two sitting chairs out front went unused. People who came to see Kane were anxious about their problem. They were in no mood to sit and wait. So, they paced.

Kane looked across his desk. Jeremy sat in the guest chair to his right. Leann occupied the one to his left. Kane moved Leann's chair back to the corner. He didn't want her presence to disturb Jeremy.

Dark décor filled the room, but LED recessed lighting made the room bright. Kane was skilled at reading facial expressions and wanted to make sure he had a clear view of his guests while he interviewed them.

Jeremy said nervously, "Mr. Kane, I have a problem."

"Why have you come to me with your problem?" Kane asked.

"Well, I don't know. I mean, you're the Problem Solver aren't you? That's how the initials behind your name on your shingle out front advertise you."

Kane flashed a quick glance in Leann's direction and sighed, "Personal Solicitor, Mr.… what's your last name?"

"Scott," Jeremy replied. "My name is Jeremy Scott."

Kane looked directly at Leann but spoke to Jeremy, "As I was saying, Mr. Scott. I'm Tyler Kane, Personal Solicitor. That's the meaning of the initials behind my name on the shingle."

Leann had a perplexed look on her face as if her entire world had crumbled. She believed everything she read about Tyler Kane on the internet. "How could they be wrong about something as basic as the meaning of PS?" She thought to herself. "How much more of the information on those web pages was inaccurate or just plain fiction?" Then she realized that at least Kane himself was a real person, and she was sitting in his office with a potential client. The thought revived her dampened spirits.

"What's the nature of your problem?" Kane continued.

Jeremy looked confused and frightened. He fidgeted his fingers and said, "Well, sir, I'm not sure where to begin."

Kane took a sip from his dark burgundy-colored coffee mug, "Why don't you try to relax by telling me a little about yourself, where you're from, what kind of work you do, if and where you attend school, things of that nature."

Kane's manner and voice eased Jeremy's nerves slightly. Jeremy said, "Well, as you know, my name is Jeremy Scott. I was born in Wichita, Kansas and lived the first nine years of my life there. My dad got a promotion in his job. With the promotion, he was transferred to Nashville to work in their main offices. We lived in a rented condo in Nashville at first. Then my folks had a house built here in Smyrna the same year."

Jeremy paused and struggled to gather his thoughts.

"And how old are you now, Mr. Scott?" Kane offered.

"Twenty, well, I will be next month."

"So, your family moved to the area and built a house here in Smyrna in 2006?"

"Yes, that's right. It was 2006," Jeremy said.

"Very well," Kane said, "please continue."

Leann made detailed notes of the conversation as Kane and Jeremy talked. Kane's former secretary was proficient at shorthand, a somewhat archaic art. Kane was pleasantly surprised when Leann told him she was proficient in the abbreviated writing style as well. Kane insisted that the initial details of his interviews get recorded accurately, and he wasn't comfortable with the practice of audio recording his guests. He felt to request such might put them further on edge and cause them to withhold potentially pertinent information either knowingly or inadvertently.

"Well," Jeremy continued, "my parents enrolled me in the local school system. I was somewhat shy and awkward as a kid. Being the new kid in town didn't help either when it came to making friends. I threw myself into my school work. As a result, I excelled in my grades and graduated high school at the top of my class. I hoped to get accepted at one of the nation's top technical schools, but something happened to thwart those plans. Then my mother got sick. I decided to attend college locally because of her illness. That way, I could continue my education and help my father care for my mother at the same time."

"I'm sorry to hear that," Kane said. "How's your mother doing now?"

"It was touch-and-go there for a while, but she's much better now. She's not completely well, but she's out of the woods. Thank you, sir."

Kane cleared his throat and sipped his coffee, "Do you have any siblings, Jeremy?"

"No sir, I'm an only child. My parents tried to have more children, but things didn't work out."

Kane decided to give Jeremy a short break from the questions and answers. He took a few moments to gather some personal information from Jeremy—full name, address, and other related things. He still didn't know why Jeremy came to him, but most of the necessary groundwork had been laid to help Jeremy feel more at ease and less guarded in sharing the information.

"Now, Jeremy, is it okay if I call you Jeremy?"

"Yes, sir."

Kane wouldn't ask Jeremy to refer to him simply as "Kane," but he felt if he referred to Jeremy by his first name it might help him feel more at ease.

Kane said in a serious but compassionate tone, "Tell me exactly why you're here."

Jeremy shuffled in his chair, "well, I live in a small neighborhood. We know all our neighbors very well. One of our neighbors, the Hensleys, left town a couple of days ago for a two-week trip to the Bahamas. They asked me to stay in their house while they were gone just to keep things tidy and make the house look lived-in. I have a childhood friend I've kept in touch with from Wichita who was planning to visit me. He was scheduled to arrive this morning. I reminded Mr. Hensley about this, and he said it was fine for my friend to stay with me in their home."

"What's this friend's name?" Kane asked.

"Roger," Jeremy said, "Roger Johnson."

"You said you reminded Mr. Hensley about Roger's visit? He already knew your friend was coming to town?"

"Yes," Jeremy answered. "As I said, all the families on our street are very close, and I haven't kept it a secret about Roger's upcoming visit. I told some of my friends about it too. They've been anxious to meet him. I'm sure all our neighbors knew he was coming and probably when he was to arrive."

"Thank you, Jeremy. Please continue," Kane said.

"Well, I took a job about a year ago in a local donut shop. I needed some spending money while in school. They had a three o'clock to six thirty a.m. shift available because they bake the donuts fresh early each morning. That was perfect for me because I really didn't need full-time work. The schedule allowed me to be free during the day to attend my classes and during the evening to study, write papers, and do my homework. I also took up jogging recently to improve my health."

"Is this job in Smyrna or Murfreesboro?" Kane asked.

"Smyrna," Jeremy replied. "Anyway, I clocked out at exactly six thirty this morning and drove straight to the Hensley's house. I got there at about six forty-five. When I entered the house, I went into the kitchen, put a bagel in the toaster, drank some juice, and went up to take a shower. I like to get the donut smell and grease out of my hair as soon as I can. After I shower, I usually watch a little television while I eat to wind down before I have to leave for my first class."

"What time does your first class begin?" Kane

asked.

"At eight thirty. I have that class every weekday morning at the same time. I usually leave around ten minutes after eight and arrive at the classroom a couple of minutes before the class begins. I'm very typical in my comings and goings. It helps keep me grounded and focused."

"Please continue," Kane said after Jeremy paused for a few seconds.

"Well, I took a quick shower and was getting dressed when I heard what turned out to be an alarm clock going off down the hallway in the Hensley's bedroom. I thought it was odd at first, but then I remembered that a lot of people leave their alarm set to go off at the same time every day. But it didn't go off yesterday morning now that I think about it.

"Anyway," Jeremy continued, "I went into the bedroom to turn the alarm off and I found this lying on the nightstand in front of the clock." Jeremy stuck a shaky hand into his front pocket, pulled out an envelope, and handed it across the desk to Kane.

Kane took the envelope and looked at it closely for any irregular markings. He found none. It was just a plain white envelope with the name "Jeremy" printed on it with a red marker. He opened the envelope and retrieved the one-page letter inside. The message was short, simple, and to the point—written in a unique cursive hand. Kane's face clouded when he read the letter. He handed it to Leann. The letter startled her. She couldn't help but verbalize the words out loud as she read,

"MR. SCOTT. YOUR FRIEND ARRIVED AT THE AIRPORT AT 6:30 A.M. ONE OF OUR MEN INTERCEPTED HIM IMMEDIATELY AND TOOK HIM HOSTAGE. IF YOU WANT TO SEE YOUR FRIEND AGAIN, DO NOT CONTACT THE POLICE. BE AT THE OUTDOOR TELEPHONE AT THE PHARMBRIGHT DRUGSTORE ON THE CORNER OF OLD NASHVILLE HIGHWAY AND SAM RIDLEY PARKWAY AT 9:30 AM TO RECEIVE FURTHER INSTRUCTIONS."

Kane said, "Have you contacted the police, Jeremy?"

"No, the letter said I shouldn't. I mean, I've heard you should always call the police no matter what, and that the police have special procedures in place to handle such situations. But I was scared and confused. I wasn't sure what to do."

"So, you came to me?" Kane asked. "You mentioned my shingle earlier, but surely something must've given you the idea to come to me before you got here and saw the shingle."

"Maybe he follows your websites, Mr. Kane," Leann offered.

"They're not my websites, Miss Walker. Those websites were posted by others—*without* my permission."

"Jeremy," Kane continued, "are you aware of the websites Miss Walker mentioned?"

"Well, yes. I mean, I haven't seen them, but I've heard other students talk about them. In fact, a man came to the donut shop this morning and started talking to me. He brought up several celebrities who live in our county. He mentioned you."

Kane folded the letter and put it back in the envelope, "I see. Miss Walker, start a file on Mr. Scott. I want this letter placed in the file. Beginning right now, I'm taking Jeremy on as a client. Is this agreeable to you Jeremy?"

"Well, I don't know. I mean, yes, of course, that's why I came to you—to see if you could help me. But I don't have much money to pay a fee."

Kane glanced at the clock on the wall above his coffee shelf. It was eight forty-five a.m. "You don't need to pay a fee, Jeremy. I just want you to be completely open and honest with me at all times. I need you to stay focused and alert throughout this affair and tell me any and all information that might be pertinent to this situation.

"Now," Kane continued in an urgent tone, "is the arrival time for Roger's flight stated accurately in the note?"

"Yes, his flight was supposed to arrive at the airport at six thirty this morning. It would take some time for him to exit the plane, grab his luggage, and probably grab a snack. Then he was supposed to get a cab and come straight to the Hensley's address. I would've already left for my class, but I planned to leave a key under the welcome mat so he could get into the house. If things went according to plan, he'd arrive an hour or so after I left and no later than nine thirty anyway. I didn't think there'd be a problem if I put the key under the mat right before I left. This was supposed to be a short day for me since the professor of my afternoon class doesn't require his students to be there for all of his lectures. That way I could get back to the house to see Roger."

"And did you call the airport to see if the flight arrived as scheduled?" Kane asked.

"Yes, I called while I drove to your office. They told me the flight arrived right on schedule, precisely at six thirty this morning."

Kane was about to ask another question when his cell phone rang. He glanced at the number on the caller ID and answered the call, "Good morning, Frank."

Jeremy and Leann sat quietly and listened to the one-sided conversation.

"Yes," Kane said.

"That *is* tragic."

"About what time?"

Kane's eyebrows rose, "Where did you say that was again?"

After a few more minutes of saying "yes" and an occasional "ummm hmmm," Kane said,

"Okay, Frank. Thank you for calling."

Frank was an old family friend of Kane's. He was very close to Kane's father when he was alive. He was in his early seventies, but his experience and expertise made it beneficial for the Criminal Investigations Division of the local Sheriff's office to keep him on the payroll for consultation and other departmental matters. Due to the nature of Kane's business, along with their close friendship, Frank kept Kane informed about any interesting activities related to the department.

Kane ended the call and casually slipped his

phone into the inside pocket of his suit jacket. He gave Jeremy a serious look, "Jeremy, you described your neighborhood as being small a few minutes ago. What did you mean by that?"

"Well," Jeremy said, "I guess I meant we live on a road that only has a few houses on it."

"How many houses?"

"Only three as a matter of fact. When you turn onto our street off the main road, our house is just up a piece on the right. The second house is about a quarter of a mile up the road on the other side of the street. The Hensley's house is a couple of hundred yards up from that on the same side of the road."

Kane rubbed his chin, "When I asked you earlier, you told me your address was one hundred four Heavenly Way?"

"Yes, that's right."

Leann said, "What's going on, Mr. Kane?"

"That was Frank on the phone. He's a friend of mine who works for the County Sheriff's office. There's been a murder. A woman was shot on her back deck."

"Oh, no! That's awful!" Leann exclaimed with a look of genuine consternation on her face.

Leann said, "Did you know her? Was she a local woman?"

Kane said, "No, I didn't know her, and, yes, she was a local woman. She lived on a street just off Rock Springs Road. One of the officers on the scene knew her and identified her as a resident of the house, a Mrs. Don Richards."

Jeremy's face tightened up into a look of bewildered fear—like a wild animal paralyzed by the headlights of an oncoming vehicle not sure whether to run right, run left, or remain still.

Kane continued, "Her address was two thirty-seven Heavenly Way. She lived right next door to the house you're staying in, Jeremy."

SIX

JEREMY AND LEANN WERE in the front room of Kane's office. Kane asked them to step out while he made a couple of phone calls. Leann sat at the secretary's desk and tried to orientate herself with what she hoped would become her permanent spot.

Someone posted on their blog that Tyler Kane's secretary got married and moved away. Leann didn't know if Mr. Kane had replaced her, but she thought it was worth the trip to his office to find out. She just hoped to get lucky enough to meet him and maybe get an interview. She never dreamed she'd be sitting in his office working on a case with him. She was ecstatic.

The news of Linda Richards' murder upset Jeremy even more. He paced the floor more rapidly than he did earlier.

Jeremy was of medium height and build. He carried a few extra pounds, but he wasn't large. His brown hair was pencil straight. It wasn't long, but it wasn't exactly short either. He didn't have the look of someone who wanted to wear his hair long. He had the look of someone who hadn't had time to get a haircut. His face sported some lengthy disorganized facial hair that struggled to form a beard. Beards were popular among young college men who either fancied themselves as intellectuals or were truly bright young men. Jeremy was, in fact, a bright young man.

Leann noticed a thoughtful look on Jeremy's face as he paced the floor. The frightened look from earlier had toned down into a concerned searching look. It reminded her of a teenage boy who'd come home one night two hours after curfew and was trying to formulate a good excuse to offer his parents as to why he was late.

Kane emerged from his office and spoke to Leann first, "I assume you have a current state-of-the-art cell phone?"

"Yes, as a matter of fact, I do," Leann said.

"It has a high-quality camera?"

"Absolutely!"

"Have you used that camera much? Do you take a lot of pictures?"

"Why, yes," Leann said. "I love to take pictures—not just casual pictures of common everyday things. I love to go out into the country and take landscapes and shots of wildflowers, creeks, streams, and old trees—things like that. I also love to go into the city and photograph historic buildings and newer ones that boast the cleverness of their designers, and I love to—"

Kane broke in, "That'll do, Miss Walker, thank

you. We're going to leave in a few moments. Make sure you take your phone with you. When we get to our destination, I want you to take pictures only when I tell you and only of the things I tell you to photograph."

Kane turned his attention to Jeremy. Jeremy's pace wasn't broken at all when Kane emerged from his office and spoke to Leann. He was in a world all to himself.

Kane spoke to him in his usual even tone, "Jeremy, you told me earlier you had to take a job to have some spending money for college. Are your parents paying for your schooling?"

"Well, most of my tuition is covered by scholarships because of my academic achievements. I can live at home with my parents for free since we're so close to campus. So, I don't have to worry about out-of-state tuition or housing fees."

"What I mean to determine," Kane continued, "is whether or not your parents are well off. Do they possess significant wealth?"

"Well, no, I wouldn't say so. I mean, we live comfortably in a large house in a nice neighborhood. My dad makes good money with his job, and he's managed it well over the years. We really don't have any debt to speak of except the home mortgage and some medical bills from my mother's illness. I wouldn't say we're wealthy though. Maybe a couple of notches above middle-class but certainly not rich."

Kane changed the subject, "How did you get here, Jeremy?"

"I drove. I have an older model sedan parked

across the street near the Train Depot."

"Okay, Jeremy," Kane said, "It's ten minutes after nine. It takes about seven minutes to drive from here to the PharmBright mentioned in the note. I want you to get in your car and head that way. Don't wait near the phone in your car when you get there. I know you're frightened and unsure about what could happen, but you need to get out of your car and stand right next to the payphone. That way, if the person who's supposed to call you is watching, he'll know you're there."

Jeremy was nervous and unsure of the instructions, "Yes, sir, but am I going by myself? Aren't you going with me?"

"No, Miss Walker and I have an urgent errand to run. But don't worry Jeremy, you won't be alone."

Kane turned his attention back to Leann. Before he spoke, he noticed Jeremy hadn't moved. He looked unsure about what he was supposed to do.

"I meant for you to leave right away, Jeremy."

"Yes, sir," Jeremy said. But he made no effort to move.

"What is it, Jeremy?" Kane said.

Jeremy said, "Well, I think there's something I should tell you."

"Jeremy, I told you earlier that I want you to tell me anything you believe might be related to this problem. But we're pressed for time right now. You need to get going. Miss Walker and I will meet you back at the Hensley's house in a couple of hours. We can continue our discussion then."

Jeremy reluctantly left Kane's office. He walked across Front Street and got into his car. He pulled onto the street, drove through the roundabout, and made his way toward Old Nashville Highway. While he drove, he wondered what Mr. Kane had meant by, "You won't be alone."

SEVEN

KANE WALKED TOWARD THE front entrance of his office, "Let's go, Leann." They walked around to a side alley next to the building and into a small parking area on the back side of the building where Kane's silver truck was parked. Kane drove through the alley and turned left onto Front Street. He headed in the same direction Jeremy went moments earlier.

They drove a couple of miles and passed Old Nashville Highway where Jeremy took a right. But Kane continued through the traffic light onto Rock Springs Road. He'd drive a few more miles and turn left onto Heavenly Way.

Kane thought about Smyrna as it was when he was growing up. It was completely different back then—not much more than a one-horse town. Someone who'd moved away from the area only twenty years earlier wouldn't recognize it. Subdivisions with houses built too close together were on every side of just about every road. Elaborate condominiums and apartment complexes filled every vacant field in town. You could find any popular restaurant you could think of off Sam Ridley Parkway near the hospital. Strip malls and other businesses had popped up on every corner. Old Nashville Highway had transformed from a two-lane country road into a bustling thoroughfare.

Kane was excited about the growth of his beloved hometown. But he loved making the drive out Rock Springs Road which ultimately connected with Rocky Fork Road. The road was narrow and curvy enough in spots to break a snake's back. Trees, fields, and creeks adorned both sides of the road. Smyrna had grown from a small town into a thriving city, but Rock Springs Road maintained its deep-south country appeal.

Leann admired the scenery. She tried to resist the urge to pull out her phone and snap a picture of an old barn while Kane contemplated the details of the interesting developments the day had presented to him. First, there was the strange young lady known as Leann Walker who magically appeared in his office as his secretary. Then, there was the normal-looking college kid with a story to tell that wasn't so normal. Now, he was en route to a house he'd never seen located on a road he'd never heard of to visit the scene of a murdered woman he'd never met.

Leann broke the silence, "Why did you ask Jeremy about his family's finances?"

Kane said, "People don't abduct adults without a good reason. Money is still one of the primary motives."

"So, you wondered if the Scotts were people of significant means—people who could pay a nice ransom for Jeremy's friend."

Kane said, "I was just eliminating the possibility. I never seriously thought someone abducted Roger to get money from Jeremy's parents. But it doesn't hurt to check it off the list. There're too many reasons why it wouldn't fit."

"Oh?" Leann said.

"Well, in the first place," Kane explained, "if someone wanted the Scotts to pay them a large ransom, why would they abduct one of Jeremy's friends whom Jeremy himself hadn't seen in several years? Why not abduct Jeremy?"

"Yes, of course, I hadn't thought of that," Leann said. "But maybe they want to collect a ransom from Roger's parents?"

"Then why would they leave a ransom note with Jeremy instead Roger's parents?"

"True," Leann said.

Kane said, "To be honest, something seems strange to me about the note Jeremy found in the Hensley's bedroom. It just happened to appear on the same morning this woman was shot on her back deck right next door to the Hensley's house where Jeremy is staying. Could that be a coincidence? And what about the peculiar handwriting the abductor wrote it in?"

"Yes," Leann observed. "The envelope had Jeremy's name printed on it with a red marker, but a fancy type of cursive was used to write the letter itself. And he used black ink instead of red."

"That's very observant of you," Kane said. His confidence in Leann was growing.

Kane changed the subject, "You mentioned earlier you wanted to be a prosecutor at one time. You no longer want to pursue that aspect of the law?"

Leann snapped a picture of an old silo, "Maybe at some point in the future I'll decide to follow that course. But I've changed my mind for now. I'd rather defend the accused."

"Why did you change your mind?"

Leann was embarrassed at the question, "To be honest," she said hesitantly, "it was because of you."

"What could I have done to make you change your mind? We don't even know each other."

"It's nothing you did on a personal level."

"Stop beating around the bush and answer the question."

"Okay, okay, there's no need to interrogate me. I'm riding down a country road in a pickup truck not sitting in the witness box," Leann said playfully. "I changed my mind when a friend told me about you and those websites."

Kane rolled his eyes.

"It's true," Leann said. "Of course, I'd heard of you before because of some stories in the local newspapers. But I had no idea you'd done so much. I got interested in you when I studied those websites. It intrigued me how you appeared out of nowhere to become a local hero and a savior to people who found themselves accused of crimes they didn't commit. But what got me thinking was that those innocent people would be behind bars right now if it hadn't been for you. It made me wonder how many other people were behind bars for crimes they didn't commit.

"During my college days," she continued, "I had the opportunity to intern with the District Attorney's office in Davidson County. I learned that prosecutors have a lot on their plate. Their dockets are overflowing with cases. To expedite them, they do one of two things—"

"For one, they offer plea bargains," Kane inserted.

"Yes, but it's the other thing that opened my eyes."

"What is that?" Kane asked. He knew the answer, but he wanted to see if Leann's answer would be the same.

"They fail to investigate all the possible leads," Leann said much to Kane's delight.

She continued, "They latch on to an early suspect. Then they run with the evidence regardless of how meager it is. And they disregard promising clues that might lead to other suspects. They dramatize the little evidence they have, blow it out of proportion, convince the jurors with emotional appeals, get their convictions, and then move on to the next case. Innocent people get sent to prison as a result. Meanwhile, the ones who committed the crimes go scot-free without being inconvenienced by so much as a brief interview with a detective."

That was the primary reason Kane hung his shingle and began to take on special clients. The legal system in the United States was one of the best in the world. From the reading of Miranda rights—to preliminary hearings—to discovery—to motions to suppress evidence—to continuances, and so forth, the criminal procedure had many safeties in place all to protect the accused.

But sadly, the safeties became like burdensome regulations to busy prosecutors with more cases than they could handle. They began taking shortcuts whenever they could—usually in the investigative aspect of the process. Kane once had a friend and business associate fall victim to such. What he saw disturbed him. It gave him the idea and incentive to become a "Personal Solicitor," as he styled himself.

"What first got me interested in the law profession," Leann continued, "was a sense of protection. Too many criminals get off too easily. I wanted to do my part to protect citizens from hardened repeat offenders by becoming a good prosecutor. Violent criminals are a danger to the general public. They need to go to prison where they belong for as long as they deserve to be there. I wanted to do my part to make that happen.

"But, now, I realize there's a completely different set of citizens that need protection—those who are accused and prosecuted for crimes they didn't commit. I read about you and wanted to meet you. I wanted to learn from you and do everything I could to help protect the ones in this category."

"So, your motive is still the same," Kane said. "You want to protect innocent citizens. But now you've decided to protect innocent citizens who are in danger of losing their freedoms and possibly their lives at the hands of the government for crimes they didn't commit."

"Exactly," Leann said.

Kane hit his left turn signal, "I think we're going to get along just fine."

While they were talking, Kane had turned left onto Heavenly Way and quickly saw Jeremy's house on the right. Then he drove a piece up the road until the trees opened up slightly on the left to reveal the front yard and driveway of the Richards' house. Emergency vehicles and police cruisers were scattered all over the wide driveway. Kane pulled his truck off the long driveway about halfway up to the house and parked on the well-groomed grass.

Kane turned to Leann before he got out of the truck, "There's one more thing I want to add to our conversation before we get out. Not all prosecutors are the way you described. Some of them are genuinely concerned about the truth. They want the real criminal caught and prosecuted, and they stick to the safeties the law has put in place.

"Also, some of those who bypass those safeties do so because of the pressure their superiors put on them to get their caseloads expedited more efficiently. They're constantly doing battle with their consciences, and they eventually leave prosecutorial work to become public defenders."

"Can I ask a question?" Leann said.

"Certainly," Kane said.

"You said the PS in your title stands for "Personal Solicitor." What exactly do you mean by 'Personal'?"

"I mean that when I take on a client, I take them on exclusively. I only take one client at a time. No exceptions. I spend all my energies on the concerns of that one client without trying to juggle the details of the problems of several clients at once.

"We just discussed how prosecutors take shortcuts because of their heavy caseloads. Defense attorneys do the same thing and for the same reason. I won't. My client is my client, singular, and I'm his personal solicitor. I won't consider taking on another client until I've fully resolved the problem of my present client."

They got out of the truck and stepped onto the Richards' lawn. Before they started toward the house, Kane said, "There's one more thing, Leann."

"What is it?" Leann asked.

"Have you ever seen a dead body?"

EIGHT

EARL WAS A LARGE, stocky, country boy. He stood six foot four inches tall and had a husky body, a barrel chest, and a well-rounded gut. Standing next to him was like standing next to a mountain. He always wore blue overalls over a black tee-shirt. A long, scraggly beard covered his face. His Tennessee accent was heavy and unmistakable. He loved to hunt, fish, and go frog gigging.

Earl's given name was Connie Randolph Blake, but nobody knew it because he didn't want them to know it. "Connie" was once a boy's name but came to be considered a girl's name over time. Earl was anything but feminine. He was the same age as Kane—forty-two years old. They grew up together in the Blackman community of Rutherford County.

When Kane and Earl were younger, they hid out in Earl's dad's shop on summer mornings and listened to a morning radio show called, "The Earl and Tyler Show." Based on that, Kane dubbed him with the nickname "Earl." It stuck. Earl was married, had a family, and owned a beautiful house on the lake in the back section of the Lake Forrest subdivision in LaVergne.

Earl was a "Good Ole Boy" who never met a stranger, and he was well-liked by everyone who knew him.

Earl also had a working knowledge of every nook and cranny in Rutherford County including every out-of-the-way back road. It was impossible to mention a single road, highway, or neighborhood without Earl knowing exactly where you were talking about.

Earl was a true intellect despite his appearance. His IQ was north of one fifty-five, and he was an expert in modern technology.

Earl sat in his truck on the far side of the parking lot of a local Mexican restaurant facing the PharmBright drugstore next door. He munched on a breakfast burrito from a local convenience store. He had camouflaged earphones on his head and a nervous, plain-looking young man in his sight.

The young man was about thirty yards across the parking lot. He stood next to a payphone attached to the back corner of the drugstore. Earl arrived there a few minutes before Jeremy, installed a listening device inside the receiver of the payphone, and parked his truck at the Mexican restaurant. Before he parked, he canvassed the surrounding area to make sure no one else had parked nearby to observe Jeremy. There were none.

Kane immediately began using Earl to do much of his legwork when he opened his firm on Front

Street three years earlier. Earl loved excitement, adventure, and mystery. He was always ready to drop any other matter to move at a moment's notice when Kane called him with a mission. Despite his outgoing nature, Earl was discreet and kept sensitive information to himself.

Kane asked Earl to listen in when Roger's abductors called Jeremy with the "further instructions" they promised in the peculiar note. He also wanted Earl to protect Jeremy's safety if the need arose.

Kane was generous when he paid Earl for his services. But Earl didn't need the money. He'd gladly run Kane's missions for free just for the excitement. The money was gravy. Earl deposited all of it into a special account set aside for his kids' college. Kane paid Earl handsomely even when Earl came back from one of his missions empty-handed—like the one he was on.

Earl fantasized about the new bass boat he'd recently ordered while he sat and watched Jeremy. He perked up with interest when Jeremy walked away from the payphone, got in his car, and drove away. Earl glanced at the clock on the console of his truck. It was ten o'clock.

The phone call Jeremy was supposed to receive from Roger's abductors never came.

NINE

TYLER KANE WAS HANDSOME in an old-fashioned sort of way. His appearance was striking and impeccable. His hair was thick, dark brown, and naturally curly. He kept it short enough to avoid the curls. It always looked the same. You could never tell when he'd had a haircut or when he needed one. It was as if his hair had grown to the perfect length and froze in place. He walked with a confident gait. It didn't come across as a strut, but it sent the message that he was someone who knew what he was doing, where he was going, and exactly how to accomplish the task he'd set out to finish. He and Leann got out of his truck at the crime scene and walked across the grass toward the Richards' house.

"Of course, I've seen a dead body before," Leann said. "I'm twenty-five years old. Don't you think I've been to a funeral?"

"This isn't a funeral, Leann. Linda Richards'

body won't be cleaned, groomed, and carefully displayed in a comfortable-looking pose in a finely-crafted coffin surrounded by beautiful flowers and lovely music. She'll be lying there in her own blood with a confused look on her face and a blank, frozen stare in her eyes."

Leann swallowed hard at the mental image.

Kane stepped onto the sidewalk just in front of the house. "Do you have your camera app open?"

"Yes, sir. Open and ready to go."

"Good, take a few pictures of the front of the house."

Leann snapped a few pictures, and they walked toward the front steps that led to the entryway of the house.

An officer stopped them, "I'm sorry folks. This is a closed crime scene." His eyes lit up with admiration. "Oh, Mr. Kane, I'm sorry. I didn't recognize you."

Kane glanced at the man's badge, "Good morning, Officer Clark. Alright if we go through?"

"Yes, sir. Sheriff Brown is on the back deck."

Kane nodded in appreciation. He turned to his left, pointed, and said, "Miss Walker, I noticed a path over to the side of the house there. Let's go around that way. Someone shot Mrs. Richard's while she was on the back porch."

Kane and Leann took the path to the back deck, passed through the gate, and went up some wooden stairs onto the deck. They surveyed the scene that unfolded before them.

Sheriff Gary Brown walked toward them with a sly smile on his face, "Hello there, Kane. I'm not surprised to see you here. How's Frank this morning?"

Sheriff Brown knew all about Frank's friendship with Kane. He also knew Frank fed Kane classified information on occasion. But the sheriff was fond of Kane. He respected Kane for the times he'd ensured justice for people who'd otherwise be rotting in a tiny prison cell for the rest of their lives for crimes they didn't commit.

The sheriff was unrelenting in enforcing not only the law but also all the rules. But he trusted Kane. He relied on Kane's discretion and often allowed him to be in places he wasn't supposed to be.

"He's doing very well," Kane said with what could almost pass as a slight grin on his ever-serious face.

"Has there been any progress on the investigation?" Kane asked, always ready to get to the heart of whatever matter was at hand.

The sheriff pointed an open hand palm up in Leann's direction, "Aren't you going to introduce me?"

"Yes, of course," Kane said. "Leann Walker, meet Gary Brown. Gary is our local sheriff and a man who has my utmost respect."

The sheriff beamed slightly at Kane's comment. He nodded casually at Leann and said with a country accent, "Miss Walker." He looked back to Kane, "I just spoke with Linda Richards' husband, Mr. Don Richards. He's all tore up. I've never seen a man so crushed in my life. Henry Tatum, one of the officers on the scene, knows the Richards fairly well. He identified the body for us. He said the

Richards are, uh, were, a model couple—still very much in love after thirty-five years of marriage."

Kane ran his sharp eyes across the deck, beyond the pool, and onto the glass shower stall just beyond Linda Richards' body.

The sheriff continued, "I can give you a rundown of everything we know so far if you'd like. We haven't been here too long. I'm sure there's plenty more to learn. But we've managed to gather quite a bit of information so far."

"That'd be great. Thank you, Gary."

The sheriff's southern drawl was a bit slower than other natives in the area, "Okay, according to her husband, Linda Richards consistently wakes up at five thirty every weekday morning. She heads out for her walk ten minutes later. She exits the back door and takes the path around the house and onto the street. She walks for about thirty minutes. Then she returns to the deck, changes into her swim gear, and swims about fifty laps in their swimming pool."

"That's rather large for a residential pool isn't it?" Kane inserted.

"Well, this is rather large for a residential house," the sheriff responded.

"So it is," Kane said.

The sheriff continued, "After she finished her swim, it appears Mrs. Richards walked across to the back corner of the deck over there, entered the glass shower stall, and took a shower. Then she stepped into the adjacent wood-sided stall to dry off and change into her robe. She evidently stepped back into the shower stall and exited through its door. One of the officers said the door's jammed in the changing room. That's probably why she exited through the shower stall. She shut the door behind her, turned around, and took a bullet in the back between the shoulder blades and directly into the heart. She probably died within a split second of being shot. We think the shooter used a sniper rifle."

Leann cringed when the sheriff described the shooting. Kane noticed.

They ambled over to the shower stall while the sheriff continued his recitation of how the deadly events unfolded.

Kane looked down at Linda Richard's body and said, "The position of the body is consistent with how you described the shooting?"

The sheriff stroked his chin, "It would seem so. It'd be difficult to know for sure though. We know someone shot her with a high-powered rifle from about eighty yards out. That could provide enough force to change the position of the body upon impact."

Kane looked doubtful. "Possibly. What makes you think it was a sniper rifle?"

"Well," the sheriff said, "you can see the two bullet holes here in the glass panels of the stall. A single bullet made both holes. The bullet entered the stall through the back panel according to our expert. Then it passed through the stall, exited through the glass of the front door panel, and into Mrs. Richards' body."

Sheriff Brown didn't refer to victims as "the victim." He thought it showed respect to refer to them by their name. He also believed that using their names reminded investigators these were real people—fellow humans whose lives were stolen from them by the ultimate thief—the murderer. It provided a powerful incentive for them to do their best work to solve the crime, find the killer, and put him on the path to the punishment he deserved.

Kane gazed across the cleared acreage south of the Richards' deck just beyond the back panel of the shower stall. He vaguely made out a house in the distance. He knew it was the Hensley's house where Jeremy was staying. The entire field was mostly clear of any trees or brush. But a small patch of trees lay about eighty yards out from the deck.

The sheriff followed Kane's eyes, "We believe the shooter perched himself in one of those trees to fire the shot. We've got a couple of men down there now to investigate that area."

"That's a reasonable conclusion," Kane said guardedly. "But wouldn't it take quite a sharpshooter to make that shot? I know the air was clear with no fog or haze this morning because I went for a run. That would give the shooter a clear shot. And there's very little wind. But that's eighty yards out. You're suggesting the shooter steadied himself on a tree branch and shot eighty yards through two densely-frosted glass panels of this shower stall and still hit Linda Richards, whom he could barely see a silhouette of, directly between the shoulder blades and into the heart—all in one shot? That's some shooter!"

"Yes," the sheriff said, "that's another reason we believe the shooter used a sniper rifle. The shooter was either a sniper or someone who's had good sniper training. A well-trained sniper can shoot a bullet through a one-inch square from a hundred yards out on a windy day."

Kane stroked his chin, "I see. The question is… why would such an advanced shooter want to take the life of a middle-aged woman who'd just finished her morning exercise on a beautiful spring morning in Middle Tennessee?"

The sheriff drawled, "That's a good question. I'd like to know the answer to it myself."

Kane turned to walk away. He shot back over his shoulder, "I intend to find that answer."

TEN

JEREMY SCOTT WAS CONFUSED and scared. He stood beside the payphone at the drug store and waited until ten o'clock for Roger's abductors to call. His mind entertained all types of possible explanations as to why the call didn't come.

"Maybe I went to the wrong PharmBright," he said to himself.

"No, that couldn't be it. I must've read that note twenty times. Mr. Kane read it too. He even knew the exact amount of time it took to drive there from his office. He wouldn't make that kind of mistake. But then it takes about the same amount of time to drive from Kane's office to the other PharmBright on the corner of Old Nashville Highway and Hazelwood Drive," he thought further disturbing himself.

"No, I'm certain the note said Sam Ridley Parkway. I wish I still had that note!"

Jeremy continued the conversation with himself,

"Maybe the abductors changed their minds and decided to go ahead and kill Roger. Or maybe they wanted to scare him and accidentally killed him. Or maybe Roger did something to anger them, and they killed him."

He drove along and continued to torture himself by devising possible explanations that always led to certain death for his abducted friend.

When Jeremy left PharmBright, he turned right off Old Nashville Highway onto Sam Ridley Parkway. He drove to a spot that comforted him—a spot he often visited to think through problems or relax and reminisce.

The movie theater on 100 Movie Way just off Industrial Boulevard was a familiar place to Jeremy—like an old friend. The theater opened a couple of years after Jeremy and his family moved to Smyrna. His father took him to see a movie every week. His mother preferred to stay at home and read romance novels. Going to the movies provided a nice father and son retreat.

Jeremy's father allowed him to go to the theater alone or with a friend when he got a little older. His father dropped him off at the theater and picked him up when the movie was over. The movie sometimes ended before his father got there. Jeremy would wait outside on the sidewalk in front of the theater.

He loved to sit on the sidewalk and watch excited people go in and out of the theater. He loved to hear friends and families talk cheerfully about the movie they were about to see or about the one they'd just seen. He loved the cool air on his face in the fall and the warm breeze on his face in the summer. He loved the scent of the night air mingled with the aroma of popcorn from inside the cinema doors. Every time he smelled popcorn, regardless of where he was, his mind traveled back to the sidewalk in front of the theater on a cool autumn night.

That's where he went when he left the drug store. He parked his car in the scarcely filled parking lot, got out, and paced back and forth from one end of the sidewalk to the other. The events of the day bewildered and frustrated him. He discussed it with himself again. He tried to focus on positive explanations for why Roger's abductors didn't call.

"Maybe, Mr. Kane figured it out already and found and freed Roger from his captors."

"No, I've heard he's good, but I doubt he's that good."

"Maybe, Roger found a way to escape. No, that's not likely."

He paced for about fifteen minutes before he gave up. He got in his car and headed back toward Heavenly Way. The clock on his phone said 10:25 a.m. He turned right off StoneCrest Boulevard onto Rock Springs Road. He could hardly believe it. It seemed like the day had lasted for an eternity, and it wasn't even eleven a.m. yet.

The late-spring day had developed into a beautiful treat. But its splendor was lost on Jeremy while he drove. He was scared—his mind clouded. He felt like he was driving through a five-mile long tunnel with no headlights.

Jeremy turned left onto Heavenly Way. The irony of the road's name in light of the day's events didn't escape him. He drove down the curved hill and passed his house on the right. He continued up the street until the Richards' house came into view on his left. His stomach churned when he saw the driveway and front yard cluttered with official vehicles. He imagined poor Mrs. Richards' lifeless body in the back of an ambulance covered from head to toe with a sheet. "Or in a body bag," he thought. Chills ran up his spine.

He noticed the mailbox when he arrived at the Hensley's driveway. He hadn't checked the mail since they left town. That was one of the things they asked him to do while they were away. He slowed to a stop, got the mail, got back into his car, and drove up the winding driveway toward the house.

He unlocked the front door and entered the spacious foyer. The foyer dramatically introduced the well-designed and meticulously decorated house. He went into the kitchen and poured himself some juice.

"What was that?" Jeremy said to himself. A scuffling sound came from the second floor of the house. He pondered the sound for a moment. More sounds followed. He heard footsteps walking slowly down the staircase in the next room. Curiosity briefly trumped fear, and during that brief moment, Jeremy placed his glass on the counter, walked out of the kitchen, went down a short hallway into the living room, and stood face to face with the source of the noises he heard.

Jeremy froze in place. He took a quick step back. Fear and confusion blanketed his face. His lips barely stuttered the nervous words, "How—when—

what are you doing here?”

ELEVEN

"OH BROTHER, WHAT'S HE doing here?" The sheriff said as he looked over Kane's shoulder. The sheriff, Kane, and Leann stood next to the shower stall on the back deck of the Hensley's house discussing the details of the tragic scene. Kane turned and saw the smug face of John Bowling approaching them.

John Bowling grew up in Rutherford County, but he worked as a Defense Attorney for several years in Southern Alabama. He recently moved back to the area and quickly became a star in the District Attorney's office.

The District Attorney suffered tremendous embarrassment from his deputies' losses against Tyler Kane. He couldn't stand the shame of being in that type of limelight again. On several cases, he'd made his arrests, gathered what everyone thought to be insurmountable evidence against the accused, and then pompously bragged to the newspaper reporters about how he'd fight to the death to ensure justice. Then Kane would sweep in at the last minute, seemingly behind the scenes, unravel all the evidence, and leave the Assistant DA appointed to prosecute the case standing in the courtroom looking like the "tough kid" on the playground who'd just been beaten up by the class bookworm.

John Bowling became the DA's star assistant after he moved back to the area. The DA got into the habit of assigning him the particularly tough cases. The DA didn't know whether or not Kane would be involved with Linda Richards' murder, but he wasn't taking any chances. He assigned John Bowling to prosecute the case *and* oversee the investigation.

Kane and Bowling attended school together growing up. Kane excelled in everything he did. He was a star baseball player, a star basketball player, and a star on the wrestling team. But Bowling always one-upped him. Kane was tall, lean, and athletic, but John Bowling was more so. Kane played second fiddle to Bowling with impeccable grace, but it didn't stop Bowling from letting his successes go to his head. He always made sure Kane knew he was the best and usually with sarcasm and braggadocio.

"How's it going, Kane?" Bowling asked with a what-do-you-think-you're-doing-here glare.

"Doing well, Bowling. Good to see you again," Kane exaggerated.

"So, what do we have here sheriff?" Bowling asked.

While Sheriff Brown repeated to Bowling the

same narrative he'd given Kane, Kane pulled Leann away and began pointing out some things he wanted her to take pictures of. Kane had asked the sheriff, and the sheriff had given the okay for Kane to take pictures. Kane was particularly interested in having several pictures made of the glass shower stall from every possible angle, both inside and out.

"Outdoor shower stalls are gross," Leann said to Kane.

"Why do you say that?" Kane asked.

"Mildew! Because they're outdoors, people don't think about the fact that mildew builds up inside of them just like it does in their indoor shower stalls. It looks like they've kept this one fairly clean, but I can still see a thin layer of mildew growing on the glass."

"I can barely see a haze," Kane said.

Leann scrunched her face, "A slight haze may as well be a mossy forest when it comes to mildew as far as I'm concerned. Gross!"

Kane and Leann moved to the other side of the deck so Leann could take a few shots of the pathway from the perspective of the deck. Kane looked across the field on the north side of the Hensley's house—the opposite side from where the shooter made the deadly shot. He thought about how that field was probably the last thing Linda Richards laid eyes on. A young, overzealous-looking detective ran up the steps and over to the glass stall where the sheriff and Bowling were talking. Kane and Leann joined them.

Bowling cut the sheriff off before he could speak. He sounded like a sarcastic bully even when he wasn't trying to. He said, "What did you find, Clemmons?"

Clemmons avoided Bowling and looked at the sheriff, "Well, sirs, there're three trees close together in the patch. The closest tree measures about eighty-three yards from this deck and the shower stall in particular. Evidence suggests that someone climbed that tree recently."

"What evidence?" Bowling barked.

Clemmons kept his eyes on the sheriff, "The tree's trunk has some fresh scuff marks in its bark. We also found some shoe imprints in the soft soil at the base of the tree."

"What type of soles?" Kane asked, bringing a clear look of contempt to the Assistant DA's face.

The officer didn't recognize Kane. He wasn't sure whether or not he should respond to his question. He finally answered after Sheriff Brown gave him a nod of approval, "This is a bit preliminary, but it looks like running shoes made the imprints, sir."

Kane's forehead creased, "Running shoes? Are you sure?"

"Well, as I said, we haven't made official tests yet, but yes, I'm quite certain they're running shoes."

"Please continue," Bowling said anxious to assert his authority.

"Well," Clemmons continued, "There's a good spot to brace oneself about mid-way up the tree. The height would put one just about level with the bullet holes in the shower stall.

"We also found this, sir." Clemmons held out a

plain black strap about ten feet long.

"What's that?" Bowling asked.

"It's a strap the shooter evidently used to steady his rifle. We found it dangling from a higher branch of the tree just above the spot where we believe he braced himself."

"Well," the sheriff said, "that certainly supports the idea that we're dealing with an experienced shooter. Most likely a sniper. That's a technique snipers use. They steady their rifle with a strap when they're shooting from precarious positions."

"Anything else," Bowling said to Clemmons. The sheriff's knowledge of snipers obviously irritated him.

"No sir, that's about it. Oh, Sheriff Brown, you wanted us to measure the distance from the patch of trees to the house next door. It's one hundred sixty-seven yards."

Leann noticed creases form on Kane's forehead when Clemmons made his last statement. Kane said to the sheriff, "Thanks for everything, Gary. We've got to go. I'll catch up with you later." He took Leann by the arm and rushed her toward the steps on the side of the deck.

Tyler Kane had something pressing on his mind.

TWELVE

KANE TURNED LEFT OUT of the Richard's driveway. He drove south toward where Heavenly Way dead-ended about a mile and a half up. If they'd finished the road, it would've connected with Rocky Fork Road at the dead end.

Kane pulled onto a narrow, curvy dirt road. Large oak trees overshadowed it on both sides. A large pickup truck with oversized wheels came into view after he rounded the second sharp curve. It was parked in a small clearing to their right. Kane pulled in several feet behind the truck and came to a stop.

Leann jumped slightly when a large bearded man emerged from the trees near the truck. The man rounded Kane's truck and approached the driver's side. Kane rolled down his window.

The man grinned widely, "Hey, Cuz. How in the world are ya?"

"Hello Earl," Kane said. "Nice meeting spot. I

suppose you've known about this little dirt road since it was cleared out."

"I knew about it before they cleared it, Cuz," Earl said with a proud gleam in his eye.

Kane chuckled, "I wouldn't be surprised."

"Leann, I'd like you to meet Earl. Earl helps with the investigation aspect of my cases."

That was all Kane was willing to share with Leann about Earl's involvement with his cases. Kane was a man of principle. So was Earl. But both of them were willing to bend the rules from time to time to ensure justice. Earl definitely had a stronger inclination to bend the rules than Kane when he was carrying out his missions. Kane rarely asked Earl about the details of how he came about his information. He certainly didn't want Leann to know about those details. If she was going to learn from him, he wanted her to learn to play by the book as closely as possible.

"Earl, this is Leann Walker," Kane continued. "She's assisting me in this matter with Jeremy Scott."

"Pleased to meet you, ma'am," Earl said in his thick but friendly Tennessee accent.

Leann noticed a slight smile on Kane's face when Earl rounded the truck and greeted him. She'd read on the websites that Kane was a serious man. After being in his presence for a few hours, she was inclined to believe the authors of those sites had gotten that piece of information right about him. He didn't come across as someone who was gloomy or depressed. On the contrary, his disposition epitomized confidence and contentment. He just treated serious matters seriously. She could see how the approach would've been beneficial in his work as a corporate lawyer.

Leann was somewhat opposite. While she took serious matters seriously, she also liked to approach every aspect of life with a measure of levity. She liked to smile and laugh a lot. She also liked to cut up on occasion. She was a cheerful person by nature. She'd decided that, while Kane trained her in his specific line of work, she'd train him to be a little more light-hearted.

Kane opened his door to get out, "Leann, would you excuse us for a few minutes?"

She saluted him with a serious military-style expression on her face, "Yes, sir."

Kane and Earl walked up a few feet and stood at the bumper of Earl's truck.

Kane spoke with an even and serious tone, "What do you have for me, Earl?"

"Well Cuz, as you know, I've had very little time to look into things, but I can at least confirm some of the information you requested."

"Let's start with Leann," Kane said.

"Everything seems to check out with her, Cuz. She was born and raised in Murfreesboro, graduated high school at the top of her class, went to law school in Nashville, and graduated at the top of her class there too. Her mother passed away when she was still a child. Her father remarried a couple of years later, quit his job, and went to work with his new wife in her real estate business."

Earl went on for a few minutes with more details about Leann Walker.

"Okay, Earl. I'm sorry, I'm pressed for time. Let's save some of the details about Leann for later. What did you learn about Jeremy Scott?"

While Kane and Earl talked, Leann observed the mismatched couple through the windshield. They were similar in height, but Earl was slightly taller. The similarities ended there. Earl was outgoing and animated. Kane was more introspect and subdued. Earl was large with a disheveled beard. Kane was lean, fit, and clean-shaven. A camouflaged cap topped Earl's shoulder-length scraggly hair. Kane's thick dark hair was clean-cut. It was short on the sides and flowed back from his forehead in a natural wave. Earl wore blue overalls over a black tee-shirt and looked as if he could leave on a moment's notice to go plow a field with his fingers. Kane wore a dark navy blue suit over a white starched dress shirt with a red unobtrusive business-like silk tie. Earl could be the poster boy for a national tractor club while Kane could easily pose on the spot for the cover of an executive magazine.

"How in the world could those two be related?" Leann thought to herself.

"Everything seems on the up-and-up with Jeremy too," Earl answered. "He was born in Wichita, Kansas, moved here with his parents when he was nine years old, attended school locally, excelled academically, won several scholarships, and, in the end, decided to attend college here in the county. He works an early morning shift every Monday through Friday at a local doughnut shop called Devilish Dunkers." Earl continued for several minutes relaying many of the details he'd learned about Jeremy Scott.

Kane was dubious about the internet, but Earl loved it. Earl dove into trading and auction sites with tremendous enthusiasm when they came along. He came from a family of barterers who sold everything from old car parts to silk bedsheets. He loved going to yard sales, flea markets, auctions, and dig stores. He started selling his finds on the internet and was so successful he decided to skip college altogether. He could've easily gotten into the university of his choice though. He made a fortune and could've retired at a young age and lived happily ever after. His vast knowledge and understanding of the intricate workings of the internet, coupled with his quick mind, also made it possible for him to find out just about anything anybody needed to know about anyone they wanted to know those things about.

"Good work Earl, thank you," Kane said. "Did you bring the audio recording?"

"There ain't no audio recording, Cuz," Earl said.

Kane's forehead creased, "Why not?"

"I couldn't record anything because there wasn't anything to record," Earl said. "I arrived at the pay phone shortly before Jeremy did. I installed the bug and parked at the Mexican restaurant next door. Jeremy pulled in, got out of his car, and started pacing in front of the phone. At ten o'clock, he got back in his car and left. He drove down to the cinema, parked his car, got out, and paced the sidewalk in front of the theater for about fifteen minutes. Then he got back in his car and headed out this way.

"The phone never rang." Earl finished.

Kane pondered the information for a few moments. He said, "He drove down to the cinema? I wonder why he did that."

"Probably just to mull things over," Earl said. "Maybe the cinema is his tree house."

"His tree house?" Kane asked.

"Yep. Remember, when we were kids, there was that old tree house on the Baxter's land back in the woods? Whenever something was bothering me, I'd go out and sit in that old tree house to mull things over. You did the same thing, Cuz."

"Yes, of course, that's probably right, Earl."

"Of course it's right, Cuz," Earl said. "Now, where do we go from here?"

"Well," Kane answered, "I'd like to have more details on Jeremy Scott *and* Leann Walker. But the information on Jeremy is more urgent right now."

"Piece of cake," Earl said, "Is that it?"

"No, I need you to find out everything you can about Don and Linda Richards too. Who were their friends, their best friends in particular? What kind of work does Don Richards do? What kind of work did Linda do—if she worked?

"I also noticed a road running parallel with Heavenly Way a couple of hundred yards behind the Richards' house. Find out what you can about the people who live on that road. Find some excuse to speak to some of them if you can. Ask if anyone happened to hear a gunshot early this morning.

"Oh, one other thing, Earl. How do you feel about paying Rabbit a visit?"

Earl made a sour face, "Couldn't I just get a root

canal done instead?"

Kane grinned, "The police believe the killer used a sniper rifle to shoot Linda Richards. I need to find out if any shady deals have gone down recently that involved a sniper rifle."

"Well, I wish there was another way to do it, but I'm afraid you're right, Cuz. Rabbit's the man who'd know such a thing.

"Sounds like I've got plenty to do," Earl continued. "I'd better go fuel up at the Chinese buffet for lunch."

One corner of Kane's mouth curled up slightly, but his tone was serious, "Yes, Earl, go have some lunch. But please understand that this matter has become very urgent. If I'm reading things right so far, our Mr. Scott may find himself arrested for murder in the very near future."

Kane and Earl were walking back to Kane's truck while Kane gave Earl those instructions. The window was still down, and Leann heard Kane make that last statement to Earl.

Kane and Leann retraced their way back down the winding dirt road. Leann asked with a serious tone, "What makes you think they'll arrest Jeremy?"

"Well, a couple of things point to one of two conclusions—Jeremy actually murdered Linda Richards, or someone has gone to a lot of trouble to make it look like he murdered her. Either way, he'll most likely be arrested. They'll place him at the top of the suspect list at the very least."

"What do you think Mr. Kane? Do you think Jeremy could've done the murder?"

"I wouldn't suspect Jeremy of the murder judging from what I know so far," Kane said. "But there's still a lot I don't know."

"What two things were you referring to that make it look as if he might be guilty?"

Kane looked thoughtful, "The time frame matches up for one. Linda Richards' morning workout schedule was meticulous. We can be pretty certain she was shot five or ten minutes after seven o'clock. Jeremy would've been at the Hensley's house during that time according to the time frame of his movements this morning. But he didn't mention hearing a shot. That's suspicious. He should've heard the shot."

"Maybe the shooter used a silencer," Leann offered.

"Not likely," Kane said. "I'm no expert on sniper shooting, but I do know silencers have a negative impact on the trajectory of the bullet as it's leaving the rifle. The killer already had a difficult shot to make given the distance and the need to shoot through two panels of thick heavily-frosted glass. He definitely wouldn't need a silencer affecting his accuracy."

"Maybe the shooter fired the shot while Jeremy was in the shower," Leann suggested. "He did say he took a shower. And according to his story, he would've been in the shower right about the time the shot was fired."

"That's true," Kane said, "I hadn't thought of

that. He said the alarm went off while he was dressing just after his shower. If we knew what time that alarm went off, we'd know just about the exact time he would've been in the shower. Did he mention what time the alarm went off?"

"No, I don't think he did."

"I'll have to remember to ask him about that," Kane said.

Leann felt good about herself. She thought of something Kane hadn't. She'd come to idolize him. She never dreamed she'd be able to offer any meaningful assistance so soon. With her confidence boosted, she continued, "What else makes Jeremy look guilty?"

"We'll have to discuss it later. The Hensley's house is just around this curve on the right."

"Okay," Leann said, "but I wanted to ask you about Earl. It's hard to believe you two are related."

"We're not related," Kane said.

"But he called you 'Cuz'," Leann said.

Kane's face brightened slightly, "Earl calls everyone 'Cuz.' Well, everyone he likes anyway."

Kane turned right into the Hensley's driveway, "Uh, oh, They're already here. It looks like our friend Mr. Bowling is going to pursue this with every ounce of energy he can muster."

Kane pulled his truck to the side of the driveway. Bowling's car and a handful of other official vehicles were already parked in the driveway. The sheriff's car was there too.

"How long has it been since we left the Richards' house?" Kane asked. Kane never wore watches, rings, bracelets, or male-type jewelry of any sort. He never could get comfortable with things being on his body. He was always aware of their presence. It annoyed him. He wore a simple gold wedding band throughout his marriage before his wife died. But even that took some getting used to.

"About an hour and fifteen minutes," Leann answered.

"A lot can happen in that amount of time," Kane said. He wished he'd gotten back to Jeremy sooner. Leann would soon realize how correct Kane was in making that statement.

THIRTEEN

KANE PARKED ABOUT HALFWAY up the Hensley's driveway. A well-groomed pathway ran across the yard toward a Victorian-style gazebo. Another pathway led from the gazebo up to the main walkway toward the front entrance of the house. Kane took that pathway after he looked in the other direction across the field toward the Richards' house. A thick tree line made it impossible to see into the field from the road. But there were no trees between the two houses except for the small patch of trees where the shooter fired the shot. Kane easily saw the patch from where he stood in the Hensley's driveway. Anyone could see it from inside the Hensley's house if they looked out a window on that side.

Kane and Leann walked along the pathway toward the gazebo. Royal Star Magnolias lined both sides. Royal Star Magnolias were his wife's favorite trees. Kane would've paused to admire the beauty and fragrance of their regal blooms any other time. But his pace was quick and urgent. Leann struggled to keep up. They approached the front entrance and encountered the same officer from the Richards' house earlier.

"Hello, Officer Clark," Kane said.

"I'm sorry, Mr. Kane. I'm afraid I can't let you through this time."

Kane's eyebrows furrowed, "Oh?"

"Mr. Bowling's orders," the officer explained. "He specifically told me not to let you in if you showed up here."

Kane's lips pursed slightly. He realized Bowling was going to make things difficult for him. "I'm afraid you don't have a choice, Officer. Jeremy Scott, the young man staying here, has retained my services. We were to meet with him here about this time."

"Well, uh…" Clark mumbled, "I'm not sure what to tell you."

"You need to tell me to go on through, Officer Clark. I'm Mr. Scott's attorney. I'm also his guest. I have every right to be here. The Assistant DA has no legal grounds whatsoever to bar me from these premises."

Officer Clark didn't know how to respond.

Kane smiled confidently, "Don't worry, Officer Clark. I'll take care of John Bowling."

"Well, ok, sir. If you say so." Clark stepped aside to let Kane and Leann enter the front door.

Kane and Leann barely had time to enter the house when John Bowling appeared from an adjacent room. "Hello, Kane," he said pompously.

"I've been having a very interesting conversation with your friend, Mr. Scott. Of course, what I've learned from him explains what you're doing here."

Kane mentally kicked himself for not getting to Jeremy sooner. He was certain Jeremy revealed everything to Bowling. Jeremy would've known about his right to say nothing without his attorney present because Bowling probably read him his Miranda rights before he spoke to him. But he'd probably fallen victim to the common misguided belief that, if he went ahead and talked, he'd come across as being cooperative and innocent, and somehow that would help him later if the police arrested him. It wouldn't. Jeremy had no way of knowing that law enforcement officers loved to capitalize on that common misconception. Without question, Bowling came across to Jeremy as merely wanting to gather some minor "innocent" details. The reason Bowling wasn't surprised to see Kane was doubtless because Jeremy had told him everything about his movements that morning including the fact he'd visited Kane's office and the reason he'd done so.

Jeremy entered the room. He saw Kane and said excitedly, "Mr. Kane, you're not going to believe it. When I got back to the house earlier—"

"They're a perfect match." Jeremy was cut off by an officer who'd entered the room and addressed Bowling.

"Oh?" Bowling said looking pleased.

"Yes, sir. There's no doubt about it. The soles of these running shoes we found in the guest bedroom upstairs, the room Mr. Scott is staying in, match perfectly with the imprints we found in the soft soil around the tree the shooter fired from."

"But that doesn't make any—" Jeremy began to say before Kane spoke up and cut him off.

"Don't say another word, Jeremy."

Another officer entered the house through the front door. He was carrying a high-powered rifle.

"What do we have here?" Bowling asked the officer.

"We found this rifle underneath the house, sir," the officer began. "We entered the crawl space through an entrance underneath the back deck. The rifle was against the front wall of the house. It was wrapped in a black plastic leaf bag and buried about a foot deep. Fresh scuff marks under the house led from the entrance of the crawl space to that particular spot. When we got to the spot, the dirt was loose. We suspected something might've been buried there recently. We also noticed a couple of partial shoe imprints under the house. They look like they might match the imprints we found around the tree the shooter fired from."

"What type of rifle is it?" Bowling asked.

"It's an M107 sniper rifle, sir."

"I see. Any identifying marks on it?"

"No, sir. None we can find. We'll have it tested for fingerprints immediately, of course. We *have* noticed that someone filed the numbers off of the gun."

Kane realized the significance of the events unfolding in front of him. He asked Bowling, "Did you bother to get warrants specifically stating the things you were looking for, and where you expected to find them?"

"Naturally," Bowling said as he held the warrants up over his head triumphantly.

"Moving fast aren't you?" Kane added.

"No good investigator worth his salt will let the grass grow under his feet," Bowling said to Kane in a derogatory tone that suggested Kane was an ignorant, inexperienced child in such matters.

Bowling barked at a nearby officer, "Officer, arrest this young man and take him away."

"On this evidence?" Kane protested. "Anyone could've planted these things."

"I don't know, Kane. It looks pretty open and shut to me," Bowling said with an arrogant sneer on his face.

"What possible reason would Jeremy Scott have for murdering Linda Richards? Where's your motive, Bowling?"

"A good prosecutor can convince a jury that the accused is guilty without any motive to speak of," Bowling responded with an obvious self-conviction that he wasn't only a good prosecutor—he was the best.

Kane said with cautious confidence, "This'll never make it past the preliminary hearing, Bowling. You'll have to convince a judge before you ever see a jury."

"Oh, yes, that's right," Bowling sneered, "you're Mr. Preliminary Hearing Man. Listen, Kane, you've done a pretty good job making a fool out of some of these local Assistant DAs around here by convincing these judges to dismiss their cases at the preliminary hearings. But you're dealing with me now." Bowling poked himself in the chest with his right thumb. "And I haven't been practicing law all these years with my eyes closed like some of these nincompoop assistant DAs you've been dealing with."

Bowling walked past Kane toward the front door. He shot over his shoulder, "See you in court, Kane. Your boy's a murderer, and I'll see to it that he pays for the crime he's committed."

Kane turned to Leann. Before he could speak, Bowling ducked his head back through the front door and said, "By the way, Kane, I'll need the note Jeremy gave you in your office this morning—the original note with the envelope. No copies. I'll send an officer by in a couple of hours to pick it up. He's not going to have any problems is he?"

"Of course not," Kane said solemnly. He realized how much Jeremy had said in his interview with Bowling. Jeremy had no idea how much trouble he'd brought on himself by naively telling Bowling those things.

Leann stood next to a silent Kane in the foyer of the Hensley's house. Everyone else had left. She was about to speak when a young man rounded the corner.

Kane said, "Who are you, young man?"

The young man looked nervous and confused. He said, "My name is Roger, sir. Roger Johnson. I'm an old friend of Jeremy's from Kansas. I arrived this morning to spend a few days with him here. What's going on? Is Jeremy in trouble?"

Leann's eyes filled with both astonishment and confusion when Roger revealed who he was.

Kane said, "Jeremy may well be in very serious trouble. And we may need your help to get him out of it. Would you be willing to help us, Roger?"

"Of course I would. Yes, of course!"

"Good," Kane said. He pulled a small writing pad and pen from his pocket. He scribbled on the top page of the pad and said, "This is the address to my office. It's just a few miles from here. Can you be there in a couple of hours?"

"Yes," Roger said, "I mean, I'd have to call a cab, but that shouldn't be a problem."

"You could use Jeremy's car," Leann offered.

"No," Kane said, "that wouldn't be a good idea. Mr. Johnson, I'll have a rental car delivered here in an hour or so. You can use the rental for the duration of your visit here in Tennessee. I'm sure the police will ask you to vacate this house during this investigation. Load all your belongings into the rental when it arrives. Then come straight to my office. I'll make arrangements for you to stay in one of our local hotels.

"We'll see you in a couple of hours, Mr. Johnson," Kane finished as he opened the front door and exited the house. Leann followed and shut the door behind her leaving a still confused Roger Johnson standing there looking down at a piece of paper with an address and a name scribbled at the bottom, "Tyler Kane, PS."

<><><>

"I don't understand," Leann said after they'd gotten into Kane's truck and pulled out of the driveway. "Is it safe to leave Roger alone? What if he's abducted again? Come to think of it, how'd he get free from his abductors in the first place? Have I missed something?"

"I suspect Roger will be perfectly safe, Leann," Kane said. "I called Earl this morning before we left my office and told him to go to the PharmBright where Jeremy was supposed to wait for the call. I wanted him to listen in on the call and watch Jeremy from a safe distance in case Jeremy ran into any danger. That call never came.

"Before the officer interrupted him about the shoes a few minutes ago, I'm pretty certain Jeremy was about to tell me that when he arrived at the Hensley's house, he found Roger there safe and sound. I'm sure Jeremy asked Roger about the abduction and how he escaped. Roger likely had no idea what he was talking about."

"Now I'm really confused," Leann said.

"Roger was never abducted," Kane said flatly. "It's become apparent that someone wanted Jeremy out of the Hensley's house at a specific time this morning. The note about his friend's abduction was how they managed to get him to leave."

"But how could they be sure Jeremy would leave at the right time? The note specifically told him not to call the police. And the phone call wouldn't have come until almost two and a half hours after Jeremy found the note. Plus, someone had already shot Linda Richards before Jeremy found the note. Why would they need for him to leave the house then?"

"Those are good questions, Leann. I think I have the answers to a couple of them. There're more questions we need answers to as well. It looks like we've got our work cut out for us. When we get back to the office, I want you to make copies of the note Jeremy gave us this morning and the envelope. Place the originals in a manila envelope and have them ready for the officer when he arrives."

"You think you'll need a copy of the note? We know what it says."

"Yes, as I said earlier, something's been bugging me about that note. It was probably a ruse to get Jeremy out of the Hensley's house, but there's something else. We need to find out what that something is and hopefully before Bowling does."

Kane remained silent for the rest of the drive back to his office. Leann could tell from the look on his face that he was concerned. It was a level of concern Kane hadn't shown in his expressions since the strange adventure began earlier that morning. She perceived that their adventure wouldn't just be the ride of her life—it would be a ride *for* Jeremy's life.

FOURTEEN

EARL DECIDED TO SKIP the Chinese buffet. He grabbed a value meal at one of the local drive-thru restaurants after his meeting with Kane. He ate while he drove back out Rock Springs Road to check out the houses on Gray Road. Gray Road ran parallel with Heavenly Way behind the Richards' house.

He turned left onto the street and directed his attention toward the houses on his right since they sat adjacent to the land lying to the back of the Richards' house. He'd begin with the fourth house on the right because it sat directly behind the Richards' house. After that, he'd check out the houses that sat behind the acreage that separated the Richards' house from the Hensley's house where the shooter fired the shot.

Earl knew the land between the Richards' house and Rock Springs Road—on the north side of the house—was clear. The land between the Richards' house and the Hensley's house was clear too. He'd also observed from Heavenly Way that the thick tree line along the side of the road made it impossible to see into those fields from the street. Getting the view from the back side of those fields as he drove down Gray Road, he saw a thick line of trees on that side of the fields as well. It would be impossible for those folks to see into those fields through the tree line from their backyards.

He approached the fourth house on the right and saw an old tractor sitting in the backyard with a considerable amount of grass growing up around it. That would give him his opening. The house, like the others on Gray Road, wasn't nearly as modern and stylish as the ones on Heavenly Way. It was a red brick basic ranch probably built in the sixties.

Earl got out of his truck and heard the baying of an old hound coming from the direction of the backyard. An older lady was working in her small garden on the south side of the house just beyond some clotheslines. He approached her, and in his friendly country manner, he said, "Hello, ma'am."

"I ain't lookin' to buy no eggs this spring," the older lady snapped without looking up from her gardening.

Earl was confused. He said, "No, ma'am. I'm not selling eggs. I wanted to ask you about that old tractor around back. Is it for sale? I might be interested in taking it off your hands."

"That ole rust bucket?" she growled. Then she realized she might be able to make a buck or two. She added quickly, "Runs like a charm. Ain't much for looks, but she won't let a feller down not even after a long day of plowin'."

"Mind if I check her out?" Earl asked.

"Knock yourself out. Here, I'll walk over with ya."

She led him along the side of the house, rounded the corner into the backyard, and walked across the large yard to the other side where the tractor was parked.

"Shut up, Sniffer!" she yelled at the hound that was still baying relentlessly. Sniffer looked old and weary, but he was determined to protect his owner against the burly intruder.

Earl noticed a small opening in the tree line as they walked across the backyard. He could vaguely make out the Richards' house in the distance across the large field. He seized the opportunity and said, "Isn't that Heavenly Way running parallel with your street over there?"

"That'd be it," the woman answered in a disinterested tone.

"I heard there was a shooting over there this morning. A woman by the name of Richards I believe."

"I ain't heard nothin' 'bout nobody being shot," the woman said.

"Yep, sure enough," Earl said as he pointed a large finger through the opening across the field behind the woman's backyard. "She got shot and killed on her back deck over yonder."

The woman stopped and faced Earl, "Killed? You mean Mrs. Richards, Mrs. Linda Richards? Dead?"

"Yes, ma'am. The police say somebody shot her

from a field right up the road a piece—the one between her house and another house over there."

"The Hensley's house," the woman said.

"I reckon so," Earl said casually. "You didn't hear any gunshots this morning?"

"I did hear a couple of shots. 'Bout two hours after sunrise," she said.

"You did?" Earl said as his interest peaked. "How many shots did you hear?"

"I said a couple!" She growled.

"Two? Are you sure it wasn't just one? There're some valleys around here. Maybe you heard an echo."

"I heard what I heard!" the woman said. "I may be old, but I ain't deaf. I figured it was them Mullins boys shootin' at squirrels again. It's a crying shame about Mrs. Richards. She was a nice enough lady and all. I must say I can't act too surprised about her gettin' herself shot though."

Earl's eyebrows rose inquisitively, "Why doesn't it surprise you that she got shot?"

"It wouldn't be the first time the big G got somebody done in."

Earl was puzzled, "The big G?"

"The big G!" She said emphatically. "Gossip, boy. Mrs. Linda Richards was a prize-winning gossip—if anybody ever had a mind to give prizes for such a thing."

"What brand of gossip did she participate in?" Earl asked. "Was it the church-social type gossip, the country-club type, or the more vicious type that could cause some real personal damage to someone?"

"Gossip is gossip!" the old lady said matter-of-factly as she turned and walked toward the tractor again. "It's all the devil's work. Ain't none of it ever done anybody a bit of good. And that Mrs. Richards was real keen on it. She was a pleasant enough woman under certain circumstances, but that tongue of hers wagged more than ole Sniffer's tail at feedin' time."

The old lady abruptly turned the conversation back to the business at hand. As she droned on about the soundness and trustworthiness of the clearly dilapidated and dysfunctional tractor, Earl tried to continue the conversation about Linda Richards.

"Do you know of anyone who was ever seriously hurt by any of Mrs. Richards' gossip?"

"Do you wanna talk about buyin' this tractor or not, boy?" The woman snapped. "I've got a garden to tend to."

"I'll tell you what," Earl said. "I'll give you one hundred dollars cash for the tractor right now if you'll answer my question about whether or not you know of anybody who's ever been seriously injured by some of Mrs. Richards' gossip."

"She's worth a hundred and twenty if she's worth a nickel," the woman said.

Earl, quite certain the old rust bucket was in fact not worth a nickel, gladly pulled out his wallet, counted out six twenty dollar bills, and said, "Sold."

The woman took the money and walked across her backyard toward her garden. She pocketed the cash, and said over her shoulder, "You'll be wantin' to talk to Johnny Ray next door."

"Oh?" Earl yelled. "About what?"

"Didn't you ask me if Mrs. Richards' gossip had ever hurt anybody?"

"Yes, ma'am."

"Well, then, I reckon you'll be wantin' to talk to Johnny Ray next door," she said as she kept walking away.

"Thank you, ma'am," Earl yelled, "I'll be back tomorrow afternoon to pick up the tractor."

"Suit yourself," she yelled as she rounded the corner of the house out of sight.

Earl eased his truck into the Rays' driveway next door. The older woman suggested that Linda Richards had spread some gossip about Johnny Ray that might've caused him some harm. Earl wondered if he was finally on track to a possible suspect.

He drove up the long driveway and could see tell-tell signs that the Rays had children. Bicycles, scooters, balls, and other kid's things cluttered the large front yard. He saw a trampoline in the side yard. Only one vehicle sat in the driveway—an old truck that looked like it was only used for duties around a farm. Earl knocked on the front door several times with no answer. He walked around and checked the backyard. He concluded that no one was home.

There was one other house on the street past the Rays' house. Earl parked his truck in the dusty driveway and saw an older man sitting on the front porch in a wooden rocker whittling. Earl stepped onto the porch, and the old man said without looking up, “Ninety-five!”

Earl didn’t know what to make of the old man’s statement. He said, “Good afternoon, sir. Ninety-five?”

“Yep,” the man said. “I’m ninety-five years old. People are always asking me how old I am. If they don’t ask, they’re wondering about it. I like to go ahead and get that out of the way. The name’s Gray, Quinton Gray. This here street was named after me,” he added with a hint of pride as he whittled away at his stick.

“Do you have a brother?” Mr. Gray asked Earl.

“No, sir. I’m an only child,” Earl answered.

“You’re the spittin’ image of that Graham boy who comes around here selling eggs a few times a year. I’d say you’ve got a couple of inches on him in height though. Good eggs too. I always buy several from him. I used to keep a few chickens out back, but I got tired of messing with them after the wife passed on. There’s nothing like fresh eggs, son. Eggs, bacon, grits, biscuits, and white country gravy at sunrise—can’t beat that.” He spoke with conviction. He clearly believed that was the breakfast of champions and his own personal secret to longevity. “And butter,” he added. “Real butter, not that yellow food-colored stuff folks buy in the stores these days.”

Finding an opening, Earl asked, “You’re usually up at sunrise?”

“I’m always up at sunrise,” Mr. Gray answered. “What’s your name, son?”

"Blake's the name, Earl Blake."

"In my ninety-five years, there've only been three days I haven't been up at sunrise, Earl. I took pneumonia when I was fourteen years old and could barely move for three full days. I get up, fix my breakfast, and eat it out on my back porch when the weather's nice."

"On your back porch, you say? Did you eat out there this morning?" Earl asked hoping to gather some meaningful information from the surprisingly talkative and energetic ninety-five-year-old.

"Nope," Gray answered. "I decided to take my breakfast in the living room this morning and listen to my old radio."

Earl tried to decide on the best approach to take. He said, "Do you know the Rays next door very well?"

Mr. Gray looked up suspiciously from his whittling, "Why? Do you have something against them?"

"Oh no, certainly not," Earl said cautiously. "I noticed an old pickup truck sitting in their driveway and was wondering if they might be willing to sell it. I stopped and knocked on the door. No one seems to be at home."

Mr. Gray resumed his whittling, "Well, the wife and kids are up in Indiana. They went to visit with some of her folks. They left out on Sunday and planned to be back by the weekend."

"Mr. Ray didn't go with them?" Earl asked.

"No, he couldn't afford to take off work. They need the money. They're in kind of a tight spot since Lily lost her job a few weeks back. What with five boys and all, things can get pretty tight trying to keep them all fed, clothed, and properly educated.

"Johnny would be at work right now." Gray continued. "He recently began working a new shift down at the car factory where he goes in at two in the afternoon and gets off at ten in the evening."

"It sounds like you know the family pretty well. They're good neighbors?" Earl asked.

"Oh yes, that Lily is a sweetheart. And those boys are all boy with their rough and rowdy ways. But they're also polite and helpful. Don't let anybody tell you there aren't still some good seeds among our young folks today. Those boys are living proof that some of our modern parents are still trying to raise well-grounded unspoiled children."

Mr. Gray continued talking. Earl decided to listen patiently and hopefully get some information that would be helpful to Kane.

"Lily comes over here with one or two of the boys about three times a week to check in on me and make sure I'm getting along alright. She usually gathers up a load of my laundry to take home and wash while she's here. She and the boys straighten up around the house too. I've never asked them for a single thing mind you. They just started doing it. She's always bringing fresh-baked pies over too. And every other week, she brings me a big pot of homemade dumplings just because she knows they're my favorite. Good folks! Such a shame they're struggling so much financially. I've offered to help out, but her husband can't get past his pride. I suppose he thinks he'd be less of a man if he took outside help to supply for his own family. The bittersweet fruit of charity is what my mama always called it.

"As far as that old truck goes," Mr. Gray continued, "Johnny might be willing to sell it. His brother gave it to him a few months back. It needs some work, and Johnny can't afford to do anything to it right now. He'd probably welcome an offer. He certainly could stand to pick up a few extra dollars."

"What happened with Mrs. Ray? Why'd she lose her job?" Earl said.

Quinton Gray grimaced, "That Richards woman happened to her job. That's one of our neighbors. She lives back behind us over there on Heavenly Way. She heard a rumor somewhere about Lily and worked her devilish magic on it like any good gossip does. She added to it, blew it all out of proportion, and then presented it as Gospel to any ear that would welcome it."

"You mean Mrs. Linda Richards, Don Richards' wife?" Earl asked knowing the answer.

"That's her. Some of these rich society women, they get bored with life. So, they get involved in some political craze to save this, that, or the other of something that isn't in danger in the first place. Or they spend their time scrounging for bits of innocent information they can spin into tasty delicacies to serve up to their highfalutin social equals."

Earl realized Mr. Gray hadn't heard about Linda Richards' murder yet. He said, "And she served up one of these delicacies about Lily Ray?"

"You bet she did! She heard something somewhere about something Lily did when she was in her teens. Nothing scandalous, mind you, but she spun that thing so hard that, by the time it reached the ears of her employer, Lily may as well have tried to blow up the local courthouse."

"Lily Ray lost her job because of the gossip? That's a little extreme isn't it?"

"Folks can be extreme these days if you haven't noticed, son."

Earl shook his head, "I've noticed."

"It's making it pretty difficult for her to find another job too." Mr. Gray added forlornly. "Johnny's beside himself over the whole thing. He wanted to go and confront Mrs. Richards, but Lily wouldn't hear of it. I think he *did* say something to Don."

Earl raised his eyebrows, "Johnny Ray knows Don that well?"

"Yes, I mean, I wouldn't say they were best buddies or anything, but they go to the range and do some shooting together from time to time."

Earl's ears perked up, "They go shooting together?"

"Yes, Johnny served as a sniper in the military. He works hard to keep his skills sharp. Beats me why he wants to do it though. I mean, he doesn't hunt at all. But I reckon a man has to have his hobby, and Johnny doesn't go for bowling, or golf, or softball, or anything like that. Would you care for some fresh iced-tea, son? I've got some out in the kitchen."

"Don't mind if I do," Earl said.

Quinton Gray moved slowly out of his chair and into the house to get the tea. Earl took the opportunity to look around outside a bit. He walked around the house and into the backyard. The older woman's house on the other side of the Rays' house was adjacent to the field directly behind the Richards' house. Quinton Gray's house sat directly behind the field where the killer fired the fatal shot. He should've easily heard the shot that morning.

Earl walked through the thick tree line so he could look across the field. He could see the patch of trees where the shooter perched himself. Quinton Gray's hearing was still excellent from what Earl could tell. The woman he'd bought the tractor from seemed pretty confident she'd heard not one but two shots that morning. Earl wanted to see if he could confirm it with Quinton Gray.

Earl made it back to the porch just before Quinton Gray emerged from the front door with the tea.

Gray nodded toward a sturdy-looking wooden chair, "Have a seat."

Earl took the glass of tea from him, "Thank you."

Earl was about to speak when they heard a single gunshot from the woods next door to Gray's house where the street dead-ended.

"Squirrels!" Mr. Gray said. "Those Mullins boys got new .22 rifles for Christmas last year. They've been terrorizing the squirrels around here ever since. They love those guns."

"The folks around here don't mind the noise?" Earl asked.

"Not really. Most of the folks around here are gun lovers anyway. The Mullins boys are responsible shooters too. They're always careful not to shoot in any direction where a bullet might hit someone or something in the background."

Earl said, "The lady who lives on the other side of the Rays up the street told me she heard some shots a couple of hours after sunrise this morning. She figured it was the Mullins boys."

"That'd be Mrs. Foster," Gray said. "Hard-boiled old woman, but she has her merits. I don't recall hearing any shots this morning." He added just as Earl was about to ask him about it.

Mr. Gray continued, "Those Mullins boys are country boys through and through. They're considerate though. I doubt they'd have gone shooting early in the morning. They'd know the noise would disturb folks."

Earl finished off the last of his tea and glanced at his watch. He rose from his chair and said, "Well, I sure do thank you for the company and the tea, Mr. Gray. I'm afraid I've got to move along."

Earl stepped off the porch and saw two teenaged boys walking toward them. He stuck around for a few more minutes to meet the Mullins boys.

Earl headed back to town after he left Quinton Gray's house. He tried to decide on where he needed to go next. The afternoon was getting away from him. He still had to do some checking on Don Richards and some of Linda Richards' friends. It looked like it'd be dark before he'd have a chance to visit with Rabbit Morris. He winced at the thought.

He summed up the details from the interviews with Mrs. Foster and Quinton Gray. Lily Ray lost her job because of some gossip Linda Richards spread about her. That was significant. It was also significant that her husband Johnny was quite upset about the matter. And it was strange that Mrs. Foster heard two shots that morning when the killer only fired once. It seemed stranger still that Mr. Gray didn't hear any shots at all that morning. The shooter fired from the field right behind his house. If Mrs. Foster heard the shots from up the street, Mr. Gray should've heard them too. He lived much closer to the spot where the shooter fired the rifle.

Earl had no way of knowing how compelling the answer to the puzzle would be when he learned it.

FIFTEEN

KANE SAT IN HIS office at 124 Front Street and made some phone calls while Leann pulled Jeremy's file and made copies of the envelope and note Jeremy found on the nightstand in the Hensley's bedroom. She got the manila envelope ready for the officer to pick up. Then she sat at her desk to write up some notes on all the things that had transpired during the investigation.

She heard the door buzzer ring after an hour or so. She looked up and saw an officer approaching her desk. She buzzed Kane to tell him the officer had arrived.

The officer stood and waited quietly without uttering a word. Kane emerged from his office about five minutes later. A heavyset woman in her mid-fifties entered the main door from the sidewalk. Kane asked the officer to inspect the contents of the manila envelope and fill out and sign a release form. The heavyset woman notarized the form, exchanged greetings with Kane, and then left. The officer took the envelope and a copy of the notarized release form and left without speaking a word.

"You could've at least managed an insincere 'Thank you,'" Leann muttered to herself as she watched the officer exit the office. To Kane, she said, "He was a little rude wasn't he?"

"Get used to it, Leann. I have a feeling we're not going to be getting any special treatment from Bowling and his men during this process."

"Shouldn't we have heard something from Roger by now?" Leann asked.

Kane glanced at the clock on the wall, "The rental place said they'd have a car out to him no later than one thirty. I suspect we'll be hearing from him very— oh, here he is now."

Leann looked out the front window. Roger was walking up the sidewalk. He entered the front office and offered a shy hello to Kane and Leann. He looked very uncertain of himself.

"Hello, Roger. I trust the rental car is satisfactory?" Kane asked.

"Yes, sir. Thank you."

"Very well, now, please join Miss Walker and me in my office," Kane said in a serious voice as he turned and entered his office and walked toward the coffee maker.

Leann and Roger got themselves situated in the two guest chairs while Kane finished pouring some coffee. He sat down at his desk and got right down to business, "Roger, I understand you and Jeremy were childhood friends in Kansas, and you continued to stay in touch after he moved to

Tennessee with his family?"

"Yes, sir."

"Have you seen him at all over the years?"

"Yes, we've been able to visit with one another on a handful of occasions."

"When was the last time you saw him previous to this visit?"

"I saw him last summer. We got a cabin at the Devil's Den State Park in Arkansas. We both love hiking and spelunking. We stayed there a couple of days and enjoyed a break from all the technology that controls so much of our lives."

Leann perceived that Kane was trying to get Roger to talk about familiar things to make him feel at ease before he moved the discussion in the direction of the unpleasant business at hand.

"Now, Roger, your flight was due to arrive at six thirty this morning. Correct?"

"Yes, sir."

"And did it arrive on schedule?"

"Yes, sir."

"And what did you do after exiting the plane?"

"I did the usual things, I suppose. I went and retrieved my luggage first. Then I ate some breakfast at one of the cafes and watched a little TV. I usually watch TV to help me wind down from a flight. I don't like to fly. I called my mom while I was watching TV to tell her my flight had landed safely. Then I took my luggage out front and got a cab."

"About what time was it when you called the cab?"

"I'd say it was about nine o'clock."

"That's a lot of television."

"There was a lot of turbulence on the flight."

Kane shifted in his chair and sipped his coffee. "You didn't have any trouble at the airport? No suspicious looking people or anything like that?"

"No, sir. None at all."

"Very well. Now, what time did you arrive at the Hensley's house?"

"Well, there wasn't much traffic. I'd say the ride took about thirty minutes or so."

"Did you notice anything suspicious when you arrived at the Hensley's house?"

"Nothing at the house. Everything seemed to be in order. I did notice the emergency vehicles at the house next door as we drove past it. I had no idea what'd happened and certainly didn't think it would involve Jeremy in any way."

"Nothing in Jeremy's recent communications with you made you think he was distressed or upset about anything?"

"No, not at all. He acted the same as always. We were both looking forward to my visit. He may have been a little excited about that, but he certainly didn't exhibit any manner I would consider out of the ordinary."

"And how did he react when he returned to the Hensley's house and found you there?"

"Shocked and maybe even a little scared when he first saw me. He looked confused."

The phone rang before Kane could ask his next question. He answered it, found out who it was, and then spoke to Roger,

"Roger, I don't think I'll need anything more

from you today. Please write down your cell phone number on that notepad beside you before you leave. Here's the name and address of the hotel where you'll be staying. Just give them your name and mention my name as well. They'll take good care of you. I want you to go ahead and try to relax and enjoy your visit as best you can under the circumstances. But please stay within Rutherford and Davidson counties just in case I need you to come in. We'll keep you informed on the progress of Jeremy's case."

"Yes, sir." Roger said, "But are you sure it's alright for me to leave Rutherford County?"

"Why wouldn't it be?" Kane asked.

"Because that detective told me not to leave the county after he interviewed me this morning."

"Mr. Bowling, the assistant DA, told you this?"

"Yes, he told me he'd probably need to speak to me again. He didn't want me to leave the county."

Kane's face took on a concerned expression, "In that case, you're correct. You shouldn't leave the county."

Roger wrote down his phone number, took the envelope from Kane with the hotel information, and left. Kane turned his attention back to the phone. "Yes Frank, what've you got for me?"

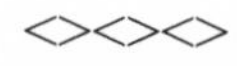

Leann waited quietly until Kane finished his call with Frank. Then she said, "We didn't get much from Roger did we?"

"I only wanted to get a couple of things from

him regarding Jeremy's behavior."

"Are you having doubts about Jeremy's innocence?"

"An accused person often tells his defense lawyer he's innocent even if he's guilty, Leann. As I told you earlier, I don't believe Jeremy committed this crime. But Jeremy's defense depends on me having no doubt whatsoever as to his innocence. If I go to court doubting Jeremy's innocence, even a little, a judge or jury could pick up on it regardless of how well I try to hide it."

Kane sipped his coffee and continued, "I wanted to know if Jeremy had acted suspiciously in recent weeks. If so, it could indicate that he was anxious or nervous about the crime he was about to commit. I also wanted to know how Jeremy reacted when he returned to the Hensley's house and found Roger there safe and sound."

"And you were satisfied with Roger's answers?"

"I believe so, yes. It seems Jeremy was genuinely surprised when he learned that Roger's abduction was a hoax."

"Why wouldn't Jeremy be surprised?" Leann asked.

"He wouldn't be surprised if he'd written the abduction note himself."

Leann cocked her head to one side and said with narrowed eyes, "I'm not following. You think Jeremy might've written the note himself and made up the story about the alarm going off which led him to find the note in the first place?"

"I don't believe that's what happened, but I've got to look at this from the prosecutor's perspective," Kane said. "Whether you want to be a prosecutor or a defense attorney, you've got to know your enemy, Leann. You've got to try and see everything from their angle. It's their perspective you'll be arguing against in the courtroom regardless of what the truth may be."

"The note was obviously a fake because Roger was at the house safe and sound. But why do you think Bowling believes Jeremy wrote it himself?" Leann asked.

"Because he arrested Jeremy for the murder."

"You're a confusing person, Mr. Kane."

Kane explained, "Bowling found the gun used to murder Linda Richards buried underneath the Hensley's house where Jeremy was staying."

Leann interrupted, "But when Bowling made the arrest, he wasn't absolutely certain it was the same gun used to kill Linda Richards."

"It was reasonable for Bowling to conclude it was the murder weapon. The soles of Jeremy's shoes matched up with the imprints they found in the dirt around the tree where the shooter fired the shot." Kane said. "They also found partial imprints underneath the house that matched the soles of those shoes too. At any rate, we know for certain *now* that the gun they found was the murder weapon. Frank just told me that ballistics confirmed it."

"This isn't looking good for Jeremy," Leann said gloomily.

Kane continued, "The only thing Jeremy had in his favor before they arrested him was the note from the abductor. Bowling knew about the note before he arrested Jeremy because Jeremy told him about it in the interview. Bowling also knew the note must've been a ruse because Roger was at the house when he got there."

A light bulb went off in Leann's head, "If Bowling thought the note was a ruse to get Jeremy out of the house, he would *have* to suspect that someone else committed the murder and wanted to get Jeremy out of the house. He wouldn't have arrested Jeremy. But he *did* arrest Jeremy. So, he does suspect Jeremy of writing the note himself."

"Bowling is clever. I'll give him that." Kane said.

"You've lost me again," Leann said.

Kane said with a thoughtful expression on his face, "You've understood my point. Bowling didn't believe that someone else wrote the abduction note and planted it in the Hensley's house for Jeremy to find. He thought Jeremy wrote the note himself so he could have an excuse to leave the house and come to see me. Bowling thinks Jeremy planned to use his visit to me as an alibi."

"But Jeremy must've been at the Hensley's house when the killer fired the shot. We've established that fact. How would the note help him?" Leann asked.

Kane said, "I noticed at the outset of this case that the timing was very tight. Judging from the time Jeremy arrived at my office this morning, he would've been very pressed for time to do the shooting, hide the gun, change his shoes and possibly his clothes, and then drive to my office. It's very tight, but it's possible. From Bowling's perspective, Jeremy was hoping the police would think the schedule was too tight, and he couldn't possibly have done all those things in the given time frame.

"But based on what Roger just told me about his being asked to remain within the county, Bowling may also be considering another possibility," Kane added.

"What's that?" Leann asked.

"He may think Jeremy had an accomplice."

Leann was startled," You think Jeremy and Roger worked together to kill Linda Richardson?"

"Of course not!" Kane said. "But Bowling may think so."

Leann began to reason out loud, "So, Bowling believes Jeremy did the shooting. Then he drove to your office shortly afterward, and then Roger came along and hid the rifle."

"He may be considering the possibility but probably not too seriously. Too many details would have to fall in place to make that scenario work. For example, if it'd happened that way, Roger would've had to go immediately to the Hensley's house from the airport to have time to hide the gun before the police arrived at the Richards' house. Although the police wouldn't show up at the Hensley's house until sometime after they began their investigation at the crime scene, they could've seen Roger crawling under the Hensley's back porch from the deck of the Richards' house. So, again, Roger would've had to get to the Hensley's house shortly after the shooting and before the police arrived at the Richards' house.

"But Roger told us that he went to retrieve his luggage when he got off the airplane. Then he went to eat some breakfast, and then he took a cab to the Hensley's house. He didn't leave the airport immediately. Someone had to sell him his breakfast, and someone had to drive the cab he took. It'd be easy to check into those things, and Roger doesn't strike me as being an imbecile. On the contrary, like Jeremy, he's a very bright young man. He would've known they'd check into those things."

"So, Bowling is counting on the tight-time-frame theory. He thinks Jeremy acted alone and hurriedly buried the gun, changed his shoes, and then left for your office with the bogus abduction note," Leann said flatly.

Kane rubbed his chin, "Yes, I believe that's what Bowling is thinking. And based on what Frank just told me, he isn't wasting any time trying to establish it."

"What did Frank tell you?"

"He told me Bowling already has a handwriting expert down at the station to examine the note the abductor left."

"And if the expert says Jeremy wrote the note, it'll seal Jeremy's fate," Leann said gloomily.

"It would seem so," Kane said matter-of-factly. "We'll know soon enough."

"Did Frank tell you anything else?" Leann asked.

"Yes, he told me Jeremy was going to be arraigned at six o'clock this evening."

"Six o'clock! There's a judge who'll do the arraignment at six o'clock this evening?"

Kane said, "Remember, the DA has placed a

high priority on this case especially since he knows I'm involved. I'll be heading out in a couple of minutes to visit with Jeremy before his arraignment. Bail will be out of the question, but I want to make sure Bowling doesn't try to cajole Jeremy into waiving his right to a preliminary hearing. Considering how Bowling is pursuing this matter, I wouldn't be surprised if the preliminary hearing was set up for next week."

"A preliminary hearing only a week after the arraignment? Isn't that unheard of?" Leann asked. "The Federal Speedy Trial Act allows for thirty days, and sometimes it goes beyond that if there are special circumstances."

"It may or may not be unheard of, but I've been fortunate enough to get my clients' cases dismissed during their preliminary hearings. As you said, those hearings usually take place several weeks after the arraignment. I've always had plenty of time to do the necessary investigations and preparations to give my clients the best representation possible. Bowling and the DA know this, and the DA is desperate to defeat me in the courtroom as if protecting his pride is more important than actual justice. He'll want to rush things along because he doesn't want me to have enough time to prepare properly."

"But that's unbelievable!" Leann exclaimed. "Jeremy deserves to have the best defense possible. Wouldn't that rob him of that defense?"

"You're forgetting a couple of things, Leann. On the one hand, the accused has the right to a speedy trial. Hence, the Speedy Trial Act you referenced a moment ago. This would certainly be fulfilling that right. On the other hand, this is just a preliminary hearing and not the actual trial. If the judge decides at the hearing that the evidence presented by the prosecution justifies a trial, Jeremy could sit behind bars for months awaiting that trial. I understand that. But that would give me ample time to prepare a defense. So, in the end, justice wouldn't have been thwarted, not from the perspective of the DA and the law anyway, even if Jeremy spends those months locked up.

Kane glanced at the clock, "I've got to get going. I need to run a couple of errands before I head over to the jail. You go on home after you finish writing up your notes. I'll brief you in the morning on how my meeting with Jeremy and the arraignment went."

"I don't think so. I'll lie awake all night wondering what happened. You give me a call later tonight. It doesn't matter how late it is."

Kane shrugged, "Suit yourself." He slid his phone into his pocket, grabbed his briefcase, and headed for the door.

One thought kept haunting Kane's mind as he drove toward Murfreesboro. It was something Leann said minutes earlier—"Then that would seal Jeremy's fate." He shuttered when he thought about how correct she may have been.

As Leann drove to her apartment, she thought about how there were only two things they could hang their hopes on at the moment. They could hope that the handwriting expert would determine that Jeremy didn't write the abduction note himself.

And more significantly, that Bowling wouldn't find a motive that pointed to Jeremy being the killer.

Bowling was correct when he said a good prosecutor could get a conviction without any hint of a motive. But that good prosecutor would have to face Tyler Kane, PS in Jeremy's case. It was her conviction that Tyler Kane wasn't just a legal star—he was a legal superstar. Undefeated and undefeatable! She had no way of knowing that, before the matter with Jeremy was over, she'd be seriously questioning her conviction.

SIXTEEN

EARL LEFT QUINTON GRAY'S house and drove to a local coffee shop to make notes on his laptop and dig for more information about Don Richards. He drove back out to Heavenly Way two hours later. He stood at the front door of Jeremy's house and rang the doorbell for the third time.

The door opened after about five minutes. The frail, slight figure of Mona Scott stood in front of him. Her meager frame spoke of the illness she'd been battling. Her eyes were red and puffy, her hair was disheveled, and her hands were trembling. But a serene and determined expression blanketed her face.

She looked up at Earl like she knew him, "Good evening, Mr. Graham. I'm sorry but—"

"No, ma'am. I'm not Mr. Graham. I'm Earl Blake. I'm working with Tyler Kane on—"

"Oh, I see," she said. "Please come in. I'm terribly sorry I'm in such a mess. I heard earlier in the day that the police had arrested Jeremy. He wasn't able to call me until a couple of hours ago. He told me Tyler Kane was acting as his lawyer. His arraignment is at six o'clock this evening, and I'm afraid I just don't have the strength to go. I'm terribly sorry I kept you waiting at the door so long."

"That's alright, ma'am," Earl said in a sympathetic voice. "I know all this must be quite a shock for you."

"I can hardly bear it," she said. "On top of it all, my husband's out of the country for a few weeks on business. I haven't been able to contact him."

They walked through the foyer toward the dining area while they talked. Earl looked to his right and saw a gun rack at the end of the hallway. The rack was divided into two sides. One was labeled "Robert" and the other one was labeled "Jeremy." Three guns were on each side. He took note of the fact that both Jeremy and his father each owned an M107 sniper rifle.

"Please have a seat here at the table, Mr. Blake. I've just made some hot tea. Would you care for some?"

"No, thank you," Earl said.

Mona Scott took a seat across the table from Earl and said, "As I mentioned, Jeremy told me Mr. Kane was representing him. He said, from what he'd heard, Mr. Kane was supposed to be some kind of wizard in criminal defense."

"Mr. Kane is very effective at what he does, ma'am. But he can only be effective if he has the information he needs. That's why I'm here."

"What kind of information are you looking for?"

"For starters, has Jeremy acted any differently over the last few weeks? Has he seemed nervous about anything?"

"Not at all. He's been a little excited about his friend Roger coming in for a visit, but certainly not nervous or fidgety about anything."

"I understand that Jeremy has been house-sitting for the Hensley's up the street. How many days has he been staying there?" Earl was asking questions he already knew the answers to. He wanted Mona Scott to get comfortable with him before he asked what was really on his mind.

"His first night was Sunday night." she answered.

Earl looked around the room and said, "You have a beautiful home, Mrs. Scott."

"Thank you. I'm afraid I can't take credit for how clean it is. I've been sick, and my husband insisted on hiring a maid. She comes every day so I don't have to spend any energy tidying up or worrying about it being dirty. In fact, she's upstairs cleaning right now."

"Mrs. Scott, when we came in I noticed a gun rack at the end of the hall."

"Yes, my husband and Jeremy love to shoot."

"Do they hunt?"

"Oh no, nothing like that. My husband was a sniper in the military. He still has a love for shooting. I'm afraid he's passed that love on to Jeremy."

"Jeremy must be a pretty good shot if a former sniper trained him," Earl said trying to sound casual so she wouldn't be upset by the possible implications of Jeremy being so good with a rifle.

"Oh yes, he's very good. His father began teaching him to shoot when he was just a child. They're both members of a local gun club. They're always bringing home trophy's they've won in shooting competitions."

"I enjoy shooting too," Earl said. "Do they shoot independently or with a team?"

"Both," Mrs. Scott said. "Sometimes they compete as father and son, but they compete with a four-man team more often."

"Who else is on their team?" Earl asked.

"Don Richards is one of them actually. The other one is a man I've never met. He lives one street over behind the Richards' house somewhere."

Earl knew she was talking about Johnny Ray. He said, "Yes, what a coincidence. Two former military snipers live right out here in the same area."

"The coincidence is even bigger than you think, Mr. Blake."

"How's that?" Earl asked.

"Don Richards is also a former military sniper."

Earl's eyebrows rose, "You mean your husband, Johnny Ray, *and* Don Richards are all former military snipers?"

"That's right. Strange, isn't it?"

Earl needed to shift the subject slightly, "Mrs. Scott, Does your husband or Jeremy own any guns other than the ones in the gun rack?"

"Yes, my husband has a couple of pistols. Those are just for protection though. He doesn't use them to compete."

"So, Both your husband and Jeremy own one sniper rifle each?"

"That's right."

"They don't have any older ones of the same model anywhere?"

"Not at all. I was surprised when Robert, that's my husband, told me how expensive they were. Not just expensive to buy but expensive to shoot. The price for ammunition is outrageous compared to that of other rifles."

"So, Jeremy wouldn't have another sniper rifle of the same model anywhere?"

"Absolutely not!" Mrs. Scott said. "What are you getting at, Mr. Blake?"

"From what I could tell, your husband and Jeremy both own M107 sniper rifles. The police found an M107 sniper rifle buried underneath the Hensley's house. They're certain it's the rifle somebody used to shoot Linda Richards with."

Kane had texted Earl earlier to tell him that the police had confirmed that the murder weapon was an M107 sniper rifle.

"Well, my husband left over a week ago. Both his and Jeremy's rifles have been hanging in that rack since. No one has touched them," she said as if it would eliminate the possibility that Jeremy could've shot Linda Richards with another rifle that she didn't know about.

Earl spoke with Mona Scott for several more minutes. He looked out the window and saw the sun setting. He said, "Mrs. Scott, I want to thank you for your time. You've been very gracious. I know you must be exhausted from this terrible day. I'd better be going."

"I should thank you, Mr. Blake. It's such a relief to know that you and Mr. Kane are handling Jeremy's case. Naturally, I want to offer as much help as I can."

They walked back to the foyer, and Earl noticed again the wooden ramp that covered the two steps going down into the entrance area. It obviously wasn't part of the original design. He commented on the fine craftsmanship of the ramp.

"Yes, it *is* nice," Mona Scott said. "I'm afraid my husband isn't very handy in building things. But Don Richards loves to work with wood. He built that beautiful deck they have around their swimming pool. My illness has kept me very weak. I struggle to climb even a couple of stairs. Don built this ramp for me last week while I was at my doctors' appointments. Now I can get to the front door easier. He's a very thoughtful friend. He also built that gun rack you saw at the end of the hallway. My husband loves it!"

"Thank you again for your time, Mrs. Scott. We'll give you a call later to let you know how Jeremy's arraignment went."

"Thank you, Mr. Blake," Mona Scott said genuinely with a concerned yet confident look on her face as she watched the kind-hearted mountain-sized man walk back to his truck.

Earl left the Scotts' house and parked his truck in the parking lot of a small country store off Rock

Springs Road. He always made detailed notes of his interviews as soon as he could while the details of the conversations were still fresh on his mind. He noted everything, even the details that didn't seem relevant.

Someone tapped on his window while he made his notes. He looked up and saw an older lady standing there. He rolled down his window to see what she wanted.

The woman saw him and said, "Oh, excuse me, sir. I thought you were Johnny."

She turned to walk away.

"Wait a minute, ma'am," Earl said. "If you don't mind me asking, you said you thought I was Johnny. Johnny who?"

"Why, Johnny Ray, of course. He drives a truck just like yours. I saw him parked in this exact spot early this morning. I *thought* it was him anyway, but I guess it was you."

"No, ma'am. I wasn't here this morning. About what time did you see the truck parked here?"

The woman laid a finger across her lips, "Well, let's see. I left my house a little after six thirty this morning. I would've driven by this store about ten minutes later."

"Are you usually out so early?" Earl asked.

"I haven't been out that early in several months," the woman said. "But I had to go to the airport to pick up my preacher's wife and bring her home. She was returning from a visit to her parents' place in Florida. Her husband had a sunrise devotional scheduled for this morning. He asked me if I could pick her up.

"Now that I think about it," the woman continued, "I *know* it was Johnny Ray's truck I saw parked here this morning. I distinctly remember seeing those little stickers on his back window. The ones shaped like little people. He has two adult ones and five children ones right across the center bottom of his back window. Yes, sir. It was definitely his truck."

"Did you stop at this store this morning, or just drive by?" Earl asked.

"I just drove by. I was running a little late. I wouldn't have had time to stop. I didn't have a reason to stop anyway."

"Could you tell if Johnny was sitting in his truck when you drove by?"

"Not that I could tell," she said. "I'd better be moving along. I'm sorry to have bothered you, young man."

"No bother at all, ma'am," Earl said. "You have a nice evening."

Earl finished writing his notes and headed back to LaVergne. He had one more stop to make, and he wasn't looking forward to it.

Rabbit Morris wasn't a desirable individual. He'd moved to the area about nine years earlier after serving a prison term. From what Earl could gather, Rabbit was involved in some deadly gang violence out in California and got a reduced sentence in exchange for some critical information on some of the gang leaders. He obviously couldn't go back to California. He chose to make his new home, such as it was, in LaVergne.

"Lucky us," Earl thought as he turned left and made his way up Old Nashville Highway toward LaVergne. Rabbit was a shady and unpleasant individual, but he'd been helpful to Earl a couple of times over the years. If anyone could shed light on a shady gun deal that involved a sniper rifle, it would be Rabbit Morris.

Earl looked at the sunset as he drove. It was almost "swallowed up by the horizon" as his grandfather used to put it. Earl hated it when he had to visit Rabbit. Going out to his place at night made things even worse. It would've been useless to go earlier in the day because Rabbit would've been sleeping. He was a creature of the night.

Rabbit lived in a small houseboat just off the lake on the southeast side of Lake Forrest Subdivision not too far from Earl's house which was on the far northwest side of the large subdivision.

Earl mulled over some of the significant things he'd learned while he drove. Linda Richards had quite a reputation as a gossip. Some of that gossip ended up getting Johnny Ray's wife fired from her job—a job her family depended on. Both Mrs. Foster and Quinton Gray indicated that Johnny was furious about it—even to the point of wanting to confront Linda Richards about the matter. According to Mr. Gray, Johnny actually said something to Don Richards about it. To top it off, Johnny once served in the military as a sniper. And Quinton Gray said Johnny worked hard to keep his shooting skills up to par. Jeremy was a well-trained shooter too, but things were beginning to look better for him in light of everything Earl learned about Johnny Ray.

"I definitely need to pay Johnny Ray a visit and ask him where he was this morning," Earl thought to himself as he turned onto a long road that led down to a dirt side-road. The dirt side-road led to Rabbit's houseboat. Quinton Gray told him that Johnny's wife and children were out of town for the week, and Johnny's vehicle hadn't been in his driveway early that morning. But the lady at the country store saw Johnny's truck parked there that morning between six thirty and seven o'clock. That store would be about a fifteen-minute walk from the spot where the killer fired the deadly shot. Johnny could've cut through the woods, and no one would've seen him walking from the store to the field between the Richards' house and the Hensley's House.

Earl turned his truck onto the dirt side-road and drove cautiously toward the spot where he'd have to get out and walk. Overhanging tree branches made the dirt road even darker. He parked his truck and entered the woods on foot. He made his way down a narrow, rugged pathway that led out to the lake where Rabbit kept his houseboat docked.

Not only was Rabbit a rough character, but the people he associated with were shady to the point of being dangerous. Earl was a big man, but he understood his limitations. He felt only slightly better as he reached down and ran his hand across the outline of the pistol he kept inside his overalls.

Earl trudged down the dark, wooded path. Some twigs crackled behind him. He spun around—spooked. He couldn't see anything in the thick darkness of the woods around him. "Probably just an animal," he thought to himself.

Chills shot up his spine before he could turn back around. He sensed a silent presence behind him. Then he felt the cold steel of a shotgun barrel press against the back of his head just above his neck.

Before Earl could blink, the pressure of the barrel intensified against his head as the man holding the gun pulled the trigger.

SEVENTEEN

JEREMY SCOTT SAT IN a small jail cell. But he wasn't alone. A chatty thirty-something-year-old man with beady eyes and arms full of cheap, faded tattoos sat across from him. The man talked non-stop. Jeremy was getting irritated.

Jeremy loved to read legal thrillers. He noticed authors loved to include jailhouse snitches in their stories. He didn't know if it happened in real life as often as those writers made it seem, but he wasn't taking any chances. He stayed silent while the tattooed man rambled on.

Jeremy had been inside a jailhouse only once in his short life. He was eleven years old. His dad had a friend who worked at the jailhouse, and this friend allowed Jeremy and his dad to visit one of the cells.

His father told him every boy and girl needed to hear those heavy iron doors slam behind them. It would leave a lasting impression on them and hopefully cause them to obey the law when they grew up. Jeremy didn't forget it. He was always careful to abide by the law to the fullest extent. He didn't want to take the slightest chance of ending up on the wrong side of those iron doors. There was only one exception. He once attended a party where a drug bust occurred. Jeremy went there to look for a friend, but as luck would have it, he arrived a couple of minutes before the raid took place. The police didn't arrest him because they believed his story. But rumors surfaced, and his reputation was slightly damaged.

Jeremy spent most of the afternoon at police headquarters before they finally allowed him to make a phone call. He already had Kane to represent him, and his father was out of the country. Naturally, he called his mother. She was devastated but encouraging.

Jeremy knew his mother wanted to be at his arraignment, but she was simply too weak to get out. He was glad she wouldn't be there because the proceedings might be too strenuous on her physical and mental state. His mother was past the worst of her illness. He didn't want to take any chances of her having a relapse. He was already worried that the news of his arrest might cause her to have a breakdown, but he felt better after he spoke to her on the phone.

He sat in his small cell and mulled those things over when the iron doors opened. An officer appeared and said in a disinterested official tone, "Scott, your lawyer's here."

<><><>

Kane walked through the front doors of the jailhouse and ran into Sheriff Brown, "Hello Gary, any news?"

"There's a couple of interesting developments," the sheriff said.

"Such as?" Kane asked.

"Well, for starters, I'm afraid they've found Jeremy's fingerprints on the rifle, Kane," the sheriff said sympathetically.

Kane mulled that over, "If Jeremy killed that woman he would've had enough sense to wipe the gun clean."

"Kane, criminals make mistakes. You know that as well as I do. A seasoned criminal could make this mistake. The fact is, he did wipe the gun clean. But one mistake murderers make when they wipe the gun clean is that they forget to wipe off any bullets that might still be in the chamber. Their fingerprints are on those bullets. Jeremy didn't make that mistake. Another common mistake is that, while they're careful to wipe off the trigger, they forget about the trigger guard. It's common for a shooter to rest his finger on the front part of the trigger guard while he's waiting for his target to arrive. He does it without being conscious of it. Then he forgets to wipe that area off later on."

"So, you found one of Jeremy's fingerprints on the front of the trigger guard," Kane said gravely.

"As clear as day," the sheriff said. "Kane, how sure are you of this boy's innocence?"

"I've still got some good reasons to believe he's innocent," Kane said. "For one, there's the suspicious abduction note. It was obviously a ruse. Somebody wanted Jeremy out of that house when the shooting took place. If Jeremy was at the Hensley's house during the time of the shooting, he might've heard the shot. He might've looked out and seen the shooter either approaching the tree or climbing out of it and walking away after he shot Linda Richards. The killer couldn't take that chance. So, he came up with a plan to get Jeremy out of the house."

"Is that all you've got, Kane?"

"There're some other considerations. But, yes, I'd say that's one of the most meaningful things I have when it comes to convincing a judge or jury."

"Then you're going to have to find some other form of meaningful evidence," the sheriff said.

Kane's eyebrows rose, "Why's that?"

"Because just a few minutes ago a handwriting expert determined 'beyond a shadow of a doubt,' as he put it, that Jeremy was the one who wrote that note."

Kane was shocked. But he didn't have time to stand around looking stunned. He said, "Gary, has Bowling looked into Don Richards?"

"Not really, and he's not inclined to do so with all the evidence implicating Jeremy. He did at least check for guns in the house. Don Richards had some guns, but they were all accounted for. No one has fired any of them recently according to the tests."

"What do *you* know about Don Richards?" Kane asked.

"I don't know him personally, but he's an

upstanding guy from everything I've heard. He's a solid businessman and a loving husband. He's also well-liked by his friends and those in the community. And he was genuinely devastated when he heard about his wife's death. No reasonable person would think that Don Richards murdered his wife. Don't count on Bowling taking a closer look at him. Bowling has tunnel vision on Jeremy right now. To be frank, I can't blame him given the evidence that keeps piling up everywhere."

"Where did Don Richards say he was this morning at the time of the murder?" Kane asked.

"He said his morning was routine. His alarm went off at six thirty. He showered, got dressed, and went down to fix himself a cup of coffee. Just before he left the house, he looked out the kitchen window and saw his wife doing her morning swim. He arrived at his office at around eight o'clock. At eight thirty, he received a phone call telling him that somebody murdered his wife."

"Who called him?"

"I called him myself," the sheriff said.

"Is there any way to substantiate that he was at the office when you called him?"

"Bowling doesn't want me wasting any time looking into him because he's convinced that Jeremy did it. But I had an officer do a little legwork inconspicuously. No one in the buildings around Don Richards' office noticed whether his vehicle had entered the parking lot or not. His office doesn't connect to any other buildings. And his secretary doesn't come in till nine o'clock. Nobody can confirm whether he was there or not. But I dialed his office number when I called him. I suppose he could've had his calls forwarded to his cell phone, but it'd take a court order to find out that information. There's no way Bowling will allow that. Even if we could confirm it, Don Richards could easily say he'd forgotten to disengage the call forwarding after he arrived at his office."

"I understand, Gary. At least Bowling hasn't found a motive. I hate to put all my eggs in one basket, but it doesn't look like I have a choice now."

"There is that, little as it is," the sheriff said. "Let's hope it holds up."

"Thanks, Gary. I'll talk to you later."

Kane walked across the foyer to check in for his visit with Jeremy. Bowling appeared through a side door out of one of the corridors and said cheerfully, "If it isn't Tyler Kane, PS. How's it going, buddy?"

Kane kept walking. He nodded slightly and said stiffly, "Bowling."

"It looks like we've got your Mr. Scott nailed down pretty good," Bowling said to Kane's back.

Kane stopped, turned, and faced Bowling. Before he could speak, Bowling continued in an exaggerated tone, "On top of everything else, we found his fingerprint on the rifle. And a handwriting expert confirmed that Jeremy wrote that bogus abduction note himself."

"I'll give you credit for being thorough, Bowling." Kane spun around and walked toward the counter.

"And we've got a motive," Bowling said with a broad grin.

Kane stopped cold and turned back around. His tone was serious, "What motive?"

"I don't have all the details from my investigator yet," Bowling said, "but it looks like Linda Richards botched up a reference she gave for Jeremy a year or so ago. Jeremy took it pretty hard from what I understand."

Kane stood silent for a moment to mull over what he'd just heard. Then he turned back around and walked to the check-in counter without saying another word. He'd already had several things he needed to speak with Jeremy about. The sheriff and Bowling just added several more to the list. They found Jeremy's fingerprints in an inconspicuous spot on the rifle. Jeremy wrote that bogus abduction letter himself according to the handwriting expert. And Bowling found a motive—a legitimate motive!

Kane finished checking in and followed the officer to the area in the back where he was to meet with Jeremy. The sheriff had asked Kane a simple but profound question. Kane walked down the corridor and began asking himself the same question,

"How sure are you of this boy's innocence?"

EIGHTEEN

RABBIT MORRIS WHOOPED AND hollered at the top of his lungs like a raving lunatic. He bent over double, stood upright again, and jumped back and forth and from side to side while he laughed wildly and screamed out quick phrases, "You should've seen the look on your face!"—more wild laughter—"I got you! I got you! You walked right into that one!"

"I ought to wring your neck you little weasel!" Earl exclaimed. He moved slowly toward Rabbit, "You could've blown my brains out."

Rabbit Morris was in his mid-fifties, but he had the energy of a seven-year-old boy. His mental capacities were in line with that age bracket as well. He was always animated and never did anything slowly. He was jumpy and his mannerisms were jerky. Anyone who experienced the displeasure of being in his presence would soon become nervous too. It wasn't possible for Rabbit to stand still when he was speaking to someone—or at any other time for that matter. He was a thin, wiry man of medium height with a slight bend in his upper back caused by the Kyphosis he inherited from his mother. His had a thin face with a receded chin. His thick, feathery beard flowed back toward his ears. His hair was thick and feathery too, and he kept it pulled back from his narrow forehead. He didn't have albinism, but his skin was abnormally white. The hair on his head and face were also a rare white color. His teeth were small and gave the appearance that he'd never lost his baby teeth. The only exception was his two upper front teeth which were inordinately large. They hung well over his bottom lip even when his mouth was closed. His eyes were a deep ebony color. If he were intentionally trying to look like a rabbit, he couldn't have done a better job at accomplishing it. When he spoke, he spat out his sentences in quick, jerky phrases.

"I knew it wasn't loaded," Rabbit said as he scurried back away from Earl. "I double-checked before I approached you. But maybe I had a right to shoot you. What are you doing out here in the middle of the night anyway?"

Earl rubbed the back of his neck, "It's only eight thirty Rabbit. That's morning for you."

"I do my best work at night-time," Rabbit spat out.

Earl didn't want to think about what type of work Rabbit went about doing at night. He said, "I need some information, Rabbit."

"About what?"

"A sniper rifle."

"That's a specialized rifle designed to shoot accurately from long distances. In the right hands, a sniper rifle can shoot that apple right off old Tom Sawyer's head from a hundred yards away."

"William Tell," Earl said.

"Will I tell you what?" Rabbit spat.

Earl shook his head, "Never mind. I know what a sniper rifle is, Rabbit. What I need to know is if someone has recently bought one in the county under shady circumstances."

"That depends," Rabbit said.

"Depends on what?"

"It depends on what's in it for me."

"I'll tell you what," Earl said, "if I'm satisfied with the information you give me, I'll refrain from ripping your arms off and using them as canoe oars."

Rabbit jumped back a couple of steps. "There's no need for threats, big Earl."

"I've just had the barrel of a shotgun pressed against the back of my head Rabbit. You're lucky I haven't twisted you into a pretzel."

"Always the gentle giant," Rabbit said. "I'll tell you what, if you can find me a new carburetor for my old fishing boat, I'll tell you everything I know."

"Fine," Earl said growing more and more impatient. He just wanted to get what he needed and get out of there.

"Well, the other night," Rabbit began.

"Which other night?" Earl interrupted. "Was it last night? Was it last week? Was it last month?"

"About two weeks ago," Rabbit said, "I was

heading over to see, uh, let's call him 'Bruce.' Anyway, I was heading over to see Bruce for, well never mind what for."

"Just get on with it Rabbit," Earl snapped.

"Okay, okay! I was going to see Bruce at his place. When I got to his house, I noticed a couple of cars parked in the front yard. I snuck up to the side window of the house and peeked in. I saw Bruce talking to a man wearing a ski mask. I thought the man was trying to rob Bruce at first, but the window was cracked open slightly. I started listening in to what they were saying."

"What did you hear?" Earl asked.

"The man must've just arrived because it sounded like the conversation had just started. The man asked Bruce if he could get him a sniper rifle. Not just any sniper rifle, he specifically wanted an M107. I don't know why though. He could've easily bought an M107 at the outdoor store or ordered one online legally and probably for a lot less money than he'd pay Bruce for one."

"Use your head, Rabbit. The man was wearing a ski mask so nobody would know who was looking to buy the rifle. He obviously wanted the rifle so he could commit a crime with it. If he bought a rifle from Bruce, it'd be clean and untraceable. There'd be no identification numbers and such like."

"Yeah, yeah, of course," Rabbit said.

"Well?" Earl said.

"Well, what?"

"Did Bruce sell the man a rifle?"

"Oh yeah, yes, Bruce went to the back of the house for a few minutes. When he came back, he was carrying an M107 sniper rifle."

"And the man left with the rifle?"

"Sure did."

"Ok, Rabbit. Do you remember anything else that might be significant? What about the cars you saw in the front yard? What kind of cars were they?"

"Beats me," Rabbit said. "It was dark. I didn't pay any attention."

"Ok, anything else?"

"You know?" Rabbit spat out.

"Do I know what?" Earl said, "You're not making any sense."

"I'd like to buy a sniper rifle, you know? It has to be an M107, you know? I need it right away, you know? I can pay you whatever you ask, you know? You know, you know, you know," Rabbit said in rapid succession. He jumped around all over the place yelling out "you know" over and over again as he bounced from one spot to another.

"What's the matter with you, Rabbit? Get hold of yourself. What in the world are you· talking about?" Earl shouted.

"The man with the ski mask who bought the gun from Bruce," Rabbit said as he continued to jump around. "He kept saying 'you know' after everything he said. It didn't matter if he was making a statement or asking a question. He always finished with 'you know.' It was weird."

Earl thought of the irony of Rabbit calling somebody weird. He rolled his eyes and turned around to leave. He shot over his shoulder, "I'm done, Rabbit. Thanks for the information."

"What about my carburetor?" Rabbit spat out.

"You think I've got one in my pocket, Rabbit? I'll get it to you when I can."

"I'll be waiting for it!" Rabbit yelled. "You better get it for me, or you'll be sorry, you know?" He skipped wildly down the path back toward his houseboat singing out "you know, you know, you know" maniacally.

Earl shook his head, started his truck and headed back up the long dark back-road. He couldn't wait to get home and put an end to the long day. It wasn't too far to his house, so he decided to wait until he got home to make his notes on his interesting visit with Rabbit.

Rabbit was a difficult person to be around, but he did come through with the necessary information. Of course, Earl suspected Rabbit got his information in a much different way than he claimed. He was probably sitting right there in the living room when the deal went down. But based on other dealings with Rabbit, Earl could at least be sure the information itself was reliable regardless of how Rabbit obtained it.

Kane assumed correctly that a sniper rifle had been bought and sold recently under shady circumstances. Time would tell if the sniper rifle "Bruce" sold to the mysterious man was related to the shooting of the Richards woman. Someone else might've bought that rifle from Bruce for something unrelated to the murder they were investigating, but based on everything Earl had learned that day, Johnny Ray or even Jeremy could've been the buyer. He'd discuss it more with Kane later. He was anxious to get home and relax in his oversized Jacuzzi.

NINETEEN

KANE ENTERED THE VISITOR'S room at the jailhouse. Jeremy was already there and seated. Kane was able to have this visit face to face across a table rather than through a thick sheet of glass because of his friendship with the sheriff.

Kane put his briefcase on the table, sat down, looked across at Jeremy, and said, "How are you holding up, Jeremy?"

"Pretty well, I suppose. I spent most of the afternoon being processed in. I've still got ink all over my fingers from where they took my fingerprints. I had no idea there was so much involved in the procedure. They finally let me make a phone call. I called my mother. She's so upset, Mr. Kane. I'm worried about her health. What's going on anyway? How could they think I could kill anybody? Especially Mrs. Richards! Why would I want any harm to come to her? The Richards are our best friends."

Kane observed Jeremy closely as he listened. He didn't have much left to convince him of Jeremy's innocence given everything he'd learned recently. Kane was highly skilled in reading people's expressions due to years of high-powered negotiating in his corporate law practice. Jeremy seemed nervous and scared, but he also came across as being confused and genuinely bewildered as to why the police would think he murdered Linda Richards.

Kane had a decision to make, and he had to make it soon. On the one hand, he could tell Jeremy he'd no longer be able to represent him. If he did that, he'd arrange for a competent replacement. Kane couldn't in good conscience defend someone he truly believed to be guilty. It wouldn't be good for him, and it wouldn't be in the best interest of the accused. On the other hand, he could believe in Jeremy's innocence absolutely and proceed with the interview. After sizing up Jeremy's present state, Kane decided on the latter option.

"Jeremy, you're still quite young, but you're a grown man nonetheless. I'll give it to you straight. Things aren't looking good. We don't have much time until the arraignment, and there are several items we need to discuss. Please try to focus and give me the answers I need without omitting any details. Even if it's something you think is insignificant, I need to know about it."

Jeremy looked frightened but tried to put on a tough front, "Yes, sir."

"Okay, now," Kane began, "I want you to give me a detailed account of all your movements this morning up until the time you arrived at my office beginning with the time you woke up. I want to hear about everyone you spoke to, where you spoke to them, and what time it was when you spoke to them. And I need to know what those conversations entailed."

Jeremy looked down and scratched the left side of his head, "My alarm went off at two thirty this morning. I washed up quickly, dressed, and grabbed a bottle of juice out of the fridge just before I left. I got into my car and left the Hensley's house at around two forty. I arrived at Devilish Dunkers at about five minutes till three."

"You forgot about the key, Jeremy," Kane said.

"The key?"

"Yes, didn't you leave a key to the Hensley's front door under the doormat before you left?" Kane asked trying to test what Jeremy would say against what he'd told him in his office earlier that morning.

"No, sir. I never put the key under the doormat. I was going to put it there just before leaving out for my first class, but everything went haywire in my mind when I found that note and learned that someone had abducted Roger. The key crossed my mind when I left the house to head to your office, but I figured it'd be useless to leave a key if someone had abducted Roger. He wouldn't need it."

"Did you find Roger waiting for you on the front porch when you got there later this morning after leaving the cinema?"

A confused look washed over Jeremy's face, "How did you know I was at the cinema?"

"A friend of mine sometimes assists me with the investigative aspect of my work. I had him observe you while you waited for the phone call from the abductors at the PharmBright drug store. He followed you for a while after you left. I needed to make sure you weren't walking into a trap. He would've kept you safe if it became necessary."

"Oh," Jeremy said. "Okay. Anyway, Roger wasn't waiting for me on the porch when I arrived at the Hensley's house. He was actually inside the house, upstairs in the room he was to stay in. He was putting his things away."

"Did it occur to you to ask him how he got into the house?"

"Yes, it did!" Jeremy said. "When I got home, I went into the kitchen to pour myself some juice. I heard some bumping around going on upstairs. I went to see what it was. When I got to the staircase, Roger was coming down the stairs! I couldn't believe it. It confused me and scared me a little too. Several questions popped into my head in rapid succession. Questions like, 'How did he get here?' 'When did he get here?' 'How did he get here so quickly?' 'Are his kidnappers here too?' 'Are they going to abduct me as well?' and 'How did he get into the house?' Nothing made any sense."

"How did he get into the house, Jeremy?" Kane asked almost wishing he hadn't told Jeremy to voice every little detail.

"He told me after he didn't find the key under the doormat he thought he'd come to the wrong house. He walked out to the mailbox to check the numbers. When the address checked out, he figured

I'd forgotten to put the key under the mat. Then he figured since he'd arrived so late he wouldn't have to wait long until I got there. He walked out to the gazebo and waited on one of the benches for a while. After five or so minutes, he got restless and decided to go around and check the back door on the deck. It was unlocked. He went on into the house, went back out the front door, got his luggage, then went upstairs and started unpacking."

"Did you leave the back door unlocked?"

"Absolutely not! I checked all the doors before I went to bed last night. I always do that even when I'm at home. I didn't use the back door after I got up this morning either. It should've been locked."

Kane ran that through his mind before he asked his next question. The back door being unlocked could explain why Jeremy's running shoes matched the imprints found in the soil surrounding the tree where the shooter fired the shot. The shooter must've entered the house through the back door, got Jeremy's shoes, and wore them when he did the shooting. After the shooting, the shooter could've crawled under the Hensley's house, buried the gun, then returned the shoes to the room where Jeremy was staying. The murderer evidently forgot to lock the back door behind him when he left the house.

Kane glanced up at the large plain-faced clock that hung on the bland, yellowish-colored cinder block wall of the small room. Time was running out. Kane still had several things he needed to discuss with Jeremy. He also needed to give him some instructions about the arraignment.

"Okay, Jeremy. We don't have much time left.

Try to finish summing up your movements of this morning. I believe you left off at the point where you'd arrived at the doughnut shop."

"Yes, I clocked in at two minutes before three and then went into the kitchen to begin doing my work. My boss was already there as usual. We said good morning to each other and went to work. After a few minutes, he went into his office to print some paperwork and get the money ready for the cash register."

Jeremy continued, "The next three hours were uneventful. It was five minutes till six before I knew it. I went to the bathroom in the back to wash my hands and arms. Then I went out front to tend to the cash register until Elizabeth began her shift at six thirty."

"In my office this morning you told me a man came in and struck up a conversation with you during this time?" Kane said.

"We usually don't have many customers during that time except for Friday mornings. But, yes, this morning, a man came in around ten minutes after six. He started talking to me about some celebrities who lived in the area. I figured he was either a visitor to the area or had just moved here. Then he started talking about you."

"Yes, you mentioned that this morning. Why did he bring me up?"

"He considered you to be one of our local celebrities. He went on about a couple of problems you'd solved that made the newspapers. He even gave me one of your cards."

Kane's eyes narrowed, "One of my cards? You

mean like a business card?"

"Yes. In fact, that was what prompted me to come to your office this morning. It was a lucky coincidence because after I found the abduction note, I was beside myself. Then I remembered your card and all the things the man told me about you. The note warned me not to call the police. I didn't know what to do. I grabbed your card, got in my car, and headed out to your office."

"That's very convenient," Kane said.

"Yes, I was certainly thankful for the coincidence."

Kane rubbed his chin, "I don't believe it was a coincidence at all."

"You don't?"

Kane said evenly, "Jeremy, I don't have any business cards. I've never used them. The man must've made some up himself on his computer using my information so he could give one to you. Either that or someone else made them up and gave the man one to give to you. Whoever left the note didn't want you calling the police, but they didn't want you waiting around at the Hensley's house either. I suspect the man who visited you at the doughnut shop wasn't interested in buying doughnuts was he?"

"Come to think it, he didn't buy anything," Jeremy said.

"That makes sense," Kane said. "That man was either an accomplice to the murder, or he was paid by the murderer to visit you without knowing why he was asked to do so. I suspect the latter. The murderer wanted you to have information about me fresh in your mind so you'd think to come to me for advice just after you found the note. I suspect the business card had my office hours printed on it?"

"It did," Jeremy said.

"Where's the card now?"

"I think it's still in my car. I probably stuck it in the sun visor above the passenger side seat when I arrived at your office. That's what I usually do with papers and such."

Kane glanced down at his notepad, "What time did the alarm clock go off in the Hensley's bedroom this morning?"

"Ten minutes after seven," Jeremy said.

"Jeremy, they found one of your fingerprints on the sniper rifle they dug up under the Hensley's house. They also confirmed that the killer used that rifle to shoot Linda Richards. Do you have any idea how your fingerprint might've ended up on it?"

Jeremy looked both shocked and frightened, "Of course not." That just doesn't make any sense. None of this makes any sense to me. Why would anyone do this to me? Why would anyone want to make it look like I murdered Mrs. Richards?"

"They might've done so if they had a vendetta against you, but I doubt that's the reason. You were probably just the most convenient choice. They needed to frame someone to keep the spotlight off themselves. It was probably nothing personal, but the results are still the same nevertheless."

"One more thing, Jeremy. Bowling found what he believes to be a motive."

"A motive!" Jeremy said in what could pass as a weak shout. "I've never even briefly entertained the idea of hurting anyone in my life much less murdering anybody."

"I didn't get many details," Kane continued, "but he said something about a reference Linda Richards was supposed to write for you a year or so ago. He said she botched it up somehow and you were pretty upset about it."

"Oh, that," Jeremy said.

"What about it, Jeremy?" Kane asked.

"Well, I applied to the technical school of my dreams. The school is strict about who they accept to the point of wanting several personal references. Mrs. Richards has known me since I was a child. She and her husband are practically my parent's best friends. It just made sense to ask her if she'd give me a reference. The school wanted the people to write their reference letter and send it to them directly rather than sending it through me. That way, there'd be no chance of me altering the references.

"Anyway," Jeremy continued, "something happened during the summer between my junior and senior years of high school. I found myself in the wrong place at the wrong time. I dropped by someone's house to pick up a friend from a party to give him a ride home. The police showed up and raided the place right after I got there. They found drugs and arrested several young people. Thankfully, they believed my story and let me go. But the news got out. Mrs. Richards got wind of it and mentioned it in her reference as a side note. The school rejected my application as a result."

"Were you upset about it?"

"Of course, I was upset about it. She didn't mean any harm by it though. She said something in the letter about me having a flawless character, and if anyone could ever say anything against me, it would be about that incident. And since I didn't actually do anything wrong, my character should still be considered flawless. Of course, it would've been best if she hadn't mentioned the incident at all, but she did, and that's that."

"And you spoke to some of your friends about the matter?"

"Only a couple of them. I guess the police must've talked to them."

"Yes, I'm sure they have," Kane said.

"This is what I was wondering if I should tell you this morning, Mr. Kane, just before you sent me out to the PharmBright to wait for the phone call from the abductors."

"I'm sorry, Jeremy. I should've let you go ahead and tell me. But it won't make any meaningful difference in the end. Assistant DA Bowling plans to move fast on this case."

Kane gave Jeremy a few instructions about the arraignment. Then an officer came into the room and told them it was time to go.

Kane offered Jeremy a few encouraging words after the arraignment was over. Then he went to his truck and sent Leann a text before he headed home. He said in the text, "*Jeremy's fingerprint found on the murder weapon. Bowling found a motive. Expert confirmed that Jeremy wrote the abduction note himself. No bail. Preliminary hearing set for Monday of next week. We'll discuss everything in the morning."*

He ran his eyes slowly over what he'd typed before he pushed send. After seeing it all spelled out, it hit him how tightly Bowling had already wrapped the noose around Jeremy's young neck. It was up to him to figure out how to cut the rope before the trap-door in the gallows flew open.

TWENTY

KANE'S ALARM WENT OFF at five o'clock the next morning. He got out of bed and did his daily exercise routine which included a five-minute plank, several pushups, several sit-ups, and a few back stretches. Then he changed into his running clothes, made himself some cold water, and left for the greenway. He ran a quick three miles, drove back home, texted Earl, showered, ate, and drove to his office at 124 Front Street in Smyrna. When he arrived there at ten minutes till seven, Leann was already there—coffee made.

"I've just decided to hire you on permanently, Miss Walker," Kane said as the comforting aroma of the freshly brewed coffee entered his nostrils.

"Really?" Leann said with excitement in her voice.

"Not really," Kane said with a slight grin forming on his face, "But you're well on your way. Let's see how this problem with Jeremy turns out.

We'll talk more about it then."

Kane was wearing a heather-gray suit with a white starched shirt accompanied by a dark purple tie with a quiet, simple pattern. Leann thought again about how impeccable he looked. She'd soon learn that Kane only wore one style of suit—a style with three rather than two buttons on the front of the suit jacket. He also had a specific color assigned to each day of the week. He wore a black suit on Mondays, a navy blue suit on Tuesdays, a heather gray suit on Wednesdays, a dark brown suit on Thursdays, and a light gray suit on Fridays.

"I can't believe the preliminary hearing is next Monday," Leann said. "That gives us less than a week to prepare."

"Yes," Kane said as he poured himself a cup of coffee. "I told you it wouldn't surprise me if Bowling rushed this thing along. It looks like I was correct in my assessment."

"After reading your text last night, it looks like things are looking worse and worse for Jeremy. In fact, they look almost impossible. Is there anything we can hang our hopes on?" Leann asked.

"There are a few things we can hope for, but nothing we can prove in court. Let's hope Earl came up with some promising leads on a suspect. He's coming by the office around nine o'clock. He has an appointment this morning with Cornelia Wells. Mrs. Wells was Linda Richards' best friend."

Kane remained in his office to tend to various matters while Leann settled into her desk out front to do some research on the internet Kane had assigned to her. It was eight forty-five when the door buzzer rang. She looked up and saw a friendly smiling face attached to a mountain in a pair of overalls.

Earl sat a large camouflaged leather bag on her desk and said, "Good morning, Miss Walker."

"Good morning, Mr. Blake," Leann said. "I'll let Mr. Kane know you're here."

The three of them got situated in Kane's office, and Kane and Earl began discussing some of the things Earl learned the previous day and that morning. He began by giving Kane the salient points of his interview with Mrs. Foster—the woman he'd bought the tractor from. He removed some pages of notes and a laptop from his bag while he talked.

"How sure was Mrs. Foster that she heard two shots instead of just one?" Kane asked.

"She was pretty certain, Cuz. She convinced me."

"And when you asked her if she knew of anyone who might've been hurt by some of Linda Richards' gossip, she mentioned a neighbor of hers by the name of Johnny Ray. Did you speak with Mr. Ray?"

"He wasn't at home," Earl said. "But I got some useful information from Quinton Gray, his next door neighbor. You'll see all this in my notes, but Gray told me that Johnny's wife lost her job due to some gossip Linda Richards spread about her. Johnny took it pretty hard. It put them in a difficult situation financially."

Kane scanned his eyes over Earl's notes, "Quinton Gray didn't hear *any* shots that morning?"

"That's what the man said. From everything I could tell, his hearing is still fine despite his age. So, it seemed strange to me that he didn't hear any shots. After all, the field where the shooter fired the rifle lies directly behind his house. Mrs. Foster's house is more than two hundred yards away from that field, and she insisted that she heard not one but two shots."

"You mentioned some boys in the area with rifles. Was Mr. Gray sure it couldn't have been the Mullins boys who fired those shots?"

"He was pretty sure. Also, just before I left his house, those boys approached him on his front porch to show off a couple of squirrels they'd shot. I asked them about it. They said they'd been staying with their grandfather on his farm in Hickman County the previous night and returned home around noon yesterday. They weren't even in town when Linda Richards was murdered."

"How could she have heard two shots? Everything suggests that the killer only fired one time," Kane mused out loud while he looked at some of the photographs Leann took of the shower stall. "That bullet clearly entered the stall through the back glass panel facing the Hensley's house. It passed through the stall, through the front glass panel, and into Linda Richards' back."

"Maybe the shooter missed the first time," Leann offered.

"Not likely," Kane said. He pointed at the pictures and added, "The shooter possessed the skill to fire a shot through two densely-frosted glass panels from eighty-plus yards away and hit Linda

Richards directly in the heart. If he'd missed the first time, I don't think he would've missed so badly he wouldn't have even hit the shower stall. And it's clear only one bullet passed through those two panels of the stall."

"Wait a minute!" Kane said looking as if a light bulb had gone off in his head.

"What is it, Cuz?" Earl said.

"No, never mind. That wouldn't make any sense at all."

"Anyway," Earl said. "Mr. Gray told me that Johnny Ray's wife and children were off visiting some of her relatives for the week. So, they haven't been home since Sunday. Johnny had to stay behind because of work. Mr. Gray also told me that Johnny works from two in the afternoon until ten at night. He also said Johnny's truck wasn't in the driveway yesterday morning at all. But I was making my notes in the parking lot of a small country store just up Rock Springs Road a piece, and a lady told me she'd seen Johnny's truck parked there that morning between six thirty and seven o'clock. Johnny could've easily walked from that store to the field next to the Hensley's house in about fifteen minutes. And he could've made that walk through the woods so no one could see him from the road."

"And Quinton Gray told you that Johnny is a former military sniper. And he's worked hard over the years to keep his skills sharp," Kane said.

"It looks like our Mr. Ray had motive, means, and opportunity," Kane added.

"How did things go with Rabbit?" Kane asked Earl. "Is he still among the living?" He added with a gleam in his eye as one corner of his mouth rose slightly.

"He's lucky he is," Earl said emphatically. "The weasel got the drop on me and put a shotgun to the back of my head and pulled the trigger. It wasn't loaded, but it gave me quite a scare."

"Did he know anything useful?" Kane asked.

"Possibly," Earl answered. "He said he saw someone buying an M107 sniper rifle from a man he called 'Bruce.' Who knows what the man's real name is."

"Did Rabbit get a good look at the man who bought the rifle?"

"No, he said the man was wearing a ski mask. He also said he didn't pay attention to what kind of car the man was driving. I guess all we got from him was that an M107 rifle was sold in the county under shady circumstances about two weeks ago."

"It's not much," Kane admitted, "and it may not even be related to Linda Richards' murder, but at least it confirmed my suspicions. It's a shame Rabbit didn't get a look at the buyer. If he could've confirmed it was Johnny Ray, we'd be in business."

"That'd be too easy, Cuz."

"How'd things go with Cornelia Wells?" Kane asked.

"Oh, I learned something very interesting from her," Earl said. "In fact, it may trump everything we know about Johnny Ray."

"Oh?"

"Well, she and Linda Richards were very close. They met every morning at nine o'clock at one of the local coffee shops. I suspect they took the opportunity to share some bits of gossip. Anyway, Mrs. Wells told me that Linda Richards had been a little upset the last couple of weeks about her husband. Nothing serious. She just felt like something wasn't right, and she couldn't put her finger on it. Mrs. Wells said she'd learned something significant about Don Richards on Monday that would explain why he'd been acting strange lately. She was planning on sharing what she'd learned with Linda Richards on Tuesday morning, but it was too late by then."

"What did Mrs. Wells learn about Don Richards?" Kane asked.

"About three weeks ago Don Richards took a weekend trip to Vegas with some of his business associates. From everything I've found in my research, Don Richards doesn't have any history of gambling to speak of. But he evidently got the weekend bug and ended up losing big in Vegas."

"How big?" Kane asked.

"He may have lost everything and then some," Earl said. "He's been liquidating assets and doing everything he can to come up with more money. He still owes over eight-hundred-thousand-dollars to a loan shark he hit up in the middle of the night while he was there."

"Eight-hundred-thousand-dollars!" Leann said. "Wow! How could someone lose that much in one weekend?"

"Remember," Earl said, "Eight-hundred-thousand-dollars is what he still owes after already paying off thousands of dollars worth of other losses."

"But how is that possible?"

"The gambling bug is dangerous," Kane said. "Especially to someone who hasn't done much gambling before, and then they suddenly head out to Vegas for a weekend. Most people who gamble regularly are accustomed to setting limits on their losses during their regular visits to gambling casinos. Let's say they set aside two hundred dollars to gamble with during a particular trip. After they've lost the two hundred dollars, they stop gambling. It helps keep them from losing everything they've got. But novices aren't familiar with the concept of placing limits on themselves before gambling. They're more easily deceived by the lure of gambling. They're drawn into the false concept that the next roll of the dice will be the big winner that will cover their losses so they can flee to their safe and stable life back home and vow never to gamble again. Don Richards wasn't a regular gambler. He didn't have this safety in place to prevent him from continuing to roll the dice."

"It's not as uncommon as you might think, Miss Walker," Earl added. "When I was in my teens, I remember my aunt telling my mom about a local doctor in her hometown who did the same kind of thing. He was a stable and trusted man, had a profitable practice, a lovely family, a beautiful house on the river, and an expensive car. He lost everything he had after a couple of days in Vegas. As a result, his wife left him. He lost her and the children as well. It drove him to drinking and that further corrupted his character. The townspeople stopped trusting him as a doctor. So, his practice went down the drain too. What a shame. A man spends his entire life working hard to build success and stability and then loses it all because of one careless tryst in Vegas."

Kane was about to speak when Earl's phone rang. Earl answered it, listened for a couple of minutes to the party at the other end, thanked them, and then hung up the phone.

"That was a friend of mine I met in a chat room several years ago. He's a private investigator out in Vegas. I called him on my drive over here and asked if he could get me some information on the loan shark Don Richards borrowed the money from."

"And?" Kane said.

"It looks like this loan shark has a particularly strong inclination toward using threats and violence to get his debtors to pay up. What do you think, Kane?"

"I think we need to make a quick trip to Vegas," Kane said.

"When?"

"Tomorrow."

"Tomorrow? That is quick."

"We're up against the clock, Earl. Jeremy's preliminary hearing is set for Monday morning at nine o'clock."

"Wow, that soon?"

Kane said, "Bowling already has all the ammunition he needs to convince a judge to send this thing to the Grand Jury. He wants to get it done before we have any real chance of figuring out how to debunk some of that ammunition.

"What else do you have for me, Earl?" Kane asked.

"I've done quite a bit of digging into Don Richards' professional life. He's the head of a successful investment club. From what I can tell, they own about eight businesses in the Middle Tennessee area." Earl handed Kane a list of the companies.

Kane ran his eyes down the list. "Let's see, a car dealership, a chain of bowling alleys, and a golf course. It looks like this investment group is pretty successful."

"Very much so," Earl said.

"What's this?" Kane asked. "SWAG."

"That stands for Siding, Windows, and Glass. It's a somewhat popular chain in Middle Tennessee that deals in those things. They started out selling wholesale to contractors. But they've opened up their business to the general public in recent years. Their home office is right here in Smyrna."

"And RoundFun, Inc?" Kane asked.

"They make and sell all types of balls. Baseballs, basketballs, golf balls, and other, uh, round things."

"Oh well, I don't see how this helps us much," Kane said. "If anything, it's just more proof of how diligent and reliable a businessman Don Richards is."

"Okay, how about Jeremy?" Kane asked. "Did you find anything more on him?"

"Well, I visited with his mother. She seemed to substantiate everything I'd learned already. Oh, it turns out his father is also a former military sniper. He's been training Jeremy since he was a boy."

"What?" Leann said excitedly.

"Yes, he and his father both own M107 sniper rifles too. They're members of a local gun club. They go to competitions all the time. They compete individually, as father and son, and also as part of a four-man team."

"Who else is on their team?" Kane asked.

"That's the kicker," Earl said. "It turns out Don Richards is also a former military sniper and to top it all off, he and Johnny Ray are the other two on the team of four with Jeremy and his father."

Kane rested his chin in his fingers, "We have three former military snipers living within a few hundred yards of each other. We also have Jeremy who's had specialized sniper training from his father, and Linda Richards was killed by a sniper rifle right there in the midst of them."

"Pretty fantastic. Huh, Cuz?"

"I'll say."

"But this makes Bowling's case against Jeremy stronger," Leann said. "Now, he can show that Jeremy was an expert with a sniper rifle. That poor boy. If he *is* innocent, I don't see how he's going to get out of this!"

They all sat silent for a few moments and pondered Leann's statement.

Earl turned his laptop around so Kane could see the screen and broke the silence, "Oh, I found this too."

"What is it?" Kane said.

"It's Jeremy's blog," Earl said.

"Jeremy has a blog?" Leann asked.

"Yes," Earl said, "and he has a somewhat unique

approach with it. He writes poetry—pretty good poetry too. He's got quite a following. He doesn't post the poetry to his blog in the normal way. He writes out his poems using a fancy style of cursive. Then he photographs what he's written and posts the images to his blog. He has hundreds of poems posted on this site."

Leann's eyes widened when she looked at the blog, "But isn't that—"

"Yes, it is," Kane interrupted. "There's no question about it. That's definitely the same unique cursive style used to write the abduction note Jeremy found in the Hensley's bedroom."

"No wonder Bowling was able to identify it so quickly. Anybody can see that Jeremy wrote that note himself," Leann said. "How certain are you that Jeremy didn't commit this murder?"

"Everybody keeps asking me that," Kane said. "Earl, see if you can get us some round-trip tickets to Vegas as soon as possible. Leann and I are going to try and catch Johnny Ray at home before he leaves out for work this afternoon. Listen, I know how bad all this looks, but I think this blog of Jeremy's may actually work in our favor."

"How's that?" Leann asked.

"I'll explain later. Let's go," Kane said as he stood up from his chair and slid his phone into his pocket.

TWENTY-ONE

KANE AND LEANN DROVE out Rock Springs Road toward Gray Road to pay a visit to Johnny Ray. They rode silently and enjoyed the scenery of the beautiful day. Leann took advantage of the silence and snapped several pictures of the country landscape to her right.

Kane turned left onto Gray Road and drove a few hundred yards until he came to Johnny Ray's house on his right. When he pulled into the driveway, he thought, "What's Earl doing here and how did he get here ahead of us?" Then he realized the truck he was seeing was, in fact, Johnny Ray's truck. He noticed another older truck parked to the side of the garage. It looked like no one had driven it for some time.

A rifle blast jarred Leann when they got out of the truck. They heard a loud commotion coming from the direction of Johnny Ray's backyard. They hurried around the house, turned the corner into the backyard, and saw a man in his mid-thirties standing next to two teenage boys holding .22 rifles. A tall, wide stack of hay bales lay about thirty yards out on the back corner of Johnny's side yard. Two old mid-sized mattresses were attached to the side of the bales that faced them, and there was a large bulls-eye target painted on the mattresses.

Johnny Ray was loudly congratulating the larger of the two boys on a shot he'd just made into the target. He was giving them shooting lessons. Kane assumed the boys were the Mullins boys Earl had mentioned.

"Good evening, Mr. Ray," Kane yelled as he and Leann approached the trio. "I'm Tyler Kane, and this is my assistant, Leann Walker."

"It's nice to meet you. My name's Johnny Ray, you know. These boys are gonna make some fine shooters, you know. Look 'there. Steven just hit that target dead center. I hope the noise didn't disturb you. In fact, I don't recall seeing y'all around here, you know. Do you live in the neighborhood?"

Johnny Ray stood about five foot nine inches in height. Except for a slight pot belly, he was in fairly decent shape. His hair was straight, slightly long, dirty blonde in color, and windblown. His eyes were blue and narrow, his skin was reddish, and his teeth were bucked and crooked with a yellowish hue. He was wearing worn-out blue jeans, an un-tucked brown button-up shirt, and a pair of brown steel-toed work shoes. Kane's first impression of Johnny Ray was that he was a simple country boy trying to enjoy an uncomplicated country life.

"No, I'm representing Jeremy Scott. The DA has

charged him with the murder of Mrs. Linda Richards. She was shot yesterday morning over behind you on Heavenly Way."

Johnny Ray looked slightly startled when Kane made his introduction. He shook his head and said, "That's a real shame, you know. Jeremy Scott has always been a good kid, you know. I know him and his dad well. We do some shooting together from time to time. Jeremy has some real talent, you know. His dad started teaching him when he was just a young boy, you know."

"Mr. Ray," Kane said, "Did you happen to hear any shots yesterday morning around seven o'clock?"

"Well, you know," Johnny said as he looked down and shuffled his feet. "I wasn't actually at home yesterday morning, you know."

"You weren't at home?" Kane asked.

"No sir, the wife is out of town with the kids. There's a great little country restaurant on the other side of Murfreesboro out Shelbyville Highway. I figured since the wife and kids were gone, I'd head on over there and get me a good breakfast, you know."

"What's the name of this restaurant?" Kane asked.

"Carla's Country Catheads. Best biscuits in the county, you know."

"What time did you go to Carla's yesterday morning?"

"Well, let's see, it was just after sunrise when I headed out. I'd say it was around five thirty or so, you know?"

"And what time did you get back home?"

Johnny seemed to search for an answer, "Well, I sat around the restaurant for a couple of hours. Then I decided to ride around a few back roads for a while. I like to do that to relax, you know. Anyway, I'd say I got back to the house at around ten o'clock. I hung around the house until about twelve o'clock. Then I headed out to get some lunch before I had to be at work at two o'clock, you know."

Kane considered asking Johnny about his wife getting fired from her job because of some gossip Linda Richards spread about her. But he thought better of it. Earl felt confident the information he'd gotten from Quinton Gray next door was reliable. There was no need to say anything to Johnny that might stir him up. After all, Johnny was an expert sniper, and there were a couple of .22 rifles within reach.

Johnny Ray seemed like a decent fellow. But the fact was, there were several things against him in Linda Richards' death including the fact that he'd just lied to Kane about his whereabouts on the morning of the murder—if Earl's information was correct. And Earl's information was almost always correct.

Kane thanked Johnny Ray for his time and walked back to his truck with Leann.

While they drove, Leann said, "The way Mr. Ray talks is a bit annoying isn't it?"

"What do you mean?" Kane asked.

"The way he kept saying 'you know' after every sentence. Didn't you notice that?"

"Yes, I did," Kane said. "A lot of folks have that

type of problem, actually. They say it without realizing they're doing so. In fact, I remember when I took my first public speaking class in college the professor taught a segment on such things. Later on, another professor taught on it too when he was teaching us how to effectively write and deliver closing arguments at the end of a trial."

"Yes," Leann said, "I remember my professor teaching that too. On one occasion, all the students were assigned to deliver their closing arguments to the class. He recorded our speeches and played them back to us. Some of the students were shocked at how many times they'd said 'you know' or some similar phrase. They had no idea they were saying those things."

"Yes," Kane said, "I remember when I was in middle school I had a Math teacher who always added the word 'okay' to everything he said. It was a running joke among the students. He didn't even say the entire word. He said it in an abbreviated way that sounded something like, 'kay."

"'kay?" Leann said.

"'kay!" Kane said.

"The human brain is complicated. To think we could say the same phrase over and over again without even realizing we're doing so. You know?" Leann said trying to produce some levity in Kane. When it didn't have any effect on him, she asked, "Do you think Johnny Ray was telling the truth about where he was yesterday morning?"

"No, I don't," Kane said. "He seemed very nervous about the questions I asked him. His responses came across as if he were trying to make them up as he went along."

"I noticed that too," Leann said.

Kane asked Leann to spend some time reading and studying Jeremy's blog when they arrived back at the office. He wanted her to search through it and write some specific things she found on there. Before she began her task, a heavyset woman in her mid-fifties entered the main door from the sidewalk carrying a small bag. The woman was to observe everything Leann did. Kane made some phone calls in his office while she worked.

Leann buzzed Kane after an hour and a half to let him know she'd finished her assignment. Kane came out of his office and read through the single sheet of paper she'd written. Kane had Leann sign the letter in the presence of the heavyset woman who'd observed her working on it. The woman notarized the letter, exchanged good afternoons with Kane, and left. Kane took the letter into his office, placed it in a file on his desk, and returned to Leann's desk.

"Johnny Ray was lying," he said.

"What's that?" Leann said.

"He told the truth about the existence of the country restaurant called Carla's Country Catheads, but he lied about having been there yesterday morning. I called and spoke to Carla herself. She knows Johnny Ray and was able to confidently say he hadn't been there yesterday morning or at any time yesterday for that matter."

"So, he definitely lied," Leann said excitedly. "This is our first big break! It certainly makes things look better for Jeremy."

"It does, but let's not get ahead of ourselves. Bowling still has an awful lot of evidence against Jeremy that we need to unravel."

Kane's phone rang. He answered it, listened for a couple of minutes, and hung up.

"That was Earl. Our flight is scheduled to leave for Las Vegas at five fifty-five tomorrow morning."

"Oh, I almost forgot about that lead. Things *are* beginning to look up." Leann said.

"Leann, it's not likely that Johnny Ray *and* a loan shark from Las Vegas murdered Linda Richards. Being murdered once is enough for anybody."

"True," Leann said, "but at least she was probably killed by one of them rather than by Jeremy. So, I'm still happy."

Leann paused for a few moments looking thoughtful, "if things seem to be pointing so heavily toward Johnny Ray being the murderer, why bother with the loan shark in Vegas? Do you think they worked in collusion with each other?"

"That would be highly unlikely," Kane said. "I still think it's best that we don't overlook any possibilities. Remember our talk about certain prosecutors who ignore other possible suspects because they think they have their killer?"

"Yes," Leann said feeling ashamed. "You're right, of course. We should look into the loan shark."

Kane went back to his office leaving a much happier Leann sitting at her desk. Once he got into his office, he sat down behind his desk and put his hand on top of the file where he'd placed the notarized letter Leann typed up. Leann thought Johnny Ray's lie about his whereabouts on the morning of the murder was their first big break in the case. As far as Kane was concerned, finding out about Jeremy's blog was their first big break.

TWENTY-TWO

KANE HATED TO SKIP his run on Thursday morning. But at least he got his other exercises in before he left out to meet Earl at his house in LaVergne. They planned to leave from there to catch their flight to Paradise, Nevada. Kane had never visited Las Vegas. Earl visited once when he took his wife to do some sightseeing several years earlier.

Kane was silent for most of the morning. He'd flown many times for business purposes, but he'd never gotten comfortable with it. There were few things he feared in life and flying was one of them. Whenever he flew, he took a good book to drown himself in throughout the flight. He took *four* good books that morning since the flight to Vegas would take over four hours—two for the flight there and two for the return flight later that evening.

Paradise, Nevada was a highly populated unincorporated area about five miles south of downtown Las Vegas. Earl's friend met them at the airport and gave them information about where they could find Ollie Malone—the loan shark who'd made the eight-hundred-thousand-dollar loan to Don Richards. According to Earl's friend, they could find Malone at a casino just a couple of miles up the road from the airport. Earl took possession of the rental car he'd reserved, and they drove straight to the casino.

Some casinos in Atlantic City closed for a few hours each day, but Las Vegas casinos stayed open twenty-four seven. It wasn't yet nine o'clock a.m. in Vegas when Kane and Earl entered the casino. There was no crowd to speak of except for a handful of bummed-out looking fellows trying futilely to strike gold on one of the many Wheel of Fortune slot machines.

Earl went to see if he could arrange a meeting with Ollie Malone. Kane wandered around the gambling area to take in the ambiance of the cavernous, well-lit, tackily decorated room. He watched a man feed what must've been his hundredth coin into the slot machine when Earl came up to him and said,

"Okay, Cuz, we're in. Now listen, when we get up there, my name is Ronny, and your name is Frank. We're visiting from Florida for a few weeks and ran across some bad luck gambling last night. Now we're tapped out and in desperate need of a loan."

Earl spoke in a hurried, whispered voice as they followed two large, well-dressed men to a discreet elevator in the back.

"Our story is that, a few weeks ago, we ran into a man named Don Richards at one of the casinos here. He recommended that we should see a man named Ollie Malone if we found ourselves losing big."

The elevator neared the penthouse. As the doors opened, Earl finished,

"That'll give us an opening to try and get some information about Don Richards."

Kane listened with an expressionless face while Earl was talking. They exited the elevator and followed their two escorts down a long lavish hallway that opened up into a large, mostly windowed, circular room. A fancy desk sat on the far side of the room and behind it sat an impeccably dressed small man with a long, narrow nose and black hair slicked back from his forehead. The man stood when they approached the desk and said in a friendly tone, "Hello, gentleman. How can I help you?"

"My name is Tyler Kane. This is my assistant Connie," Kane said in his let's-get-down-to-business voice. Earl shook his head and buried his face in one of his large hands.

Kane continued, "I'm an attorney and am presently involved in a case related to the murder of Linda Richards—the wife of a businessman named Don Richards who lives in the same town as us near Nashville, Tennessee."

Ollie turned and walked toward a bar near his desk, "Well, well Mr. Kane. Straightforward and to the point. I like that. Can I offer you a drink of some kind?"

"No thanks," Kane said, "I understand that Don Richards came to you a few weeks ago to borrow a sum of money."

"Perhaps," Malone said guardedly. "Did you say somebody murdered his wife recently? Such a shame, I'll have to send him a sympathy card," he added with mock sadness.

"How much money did you loan Mr. Richards?" Kane asked.

"*If* I loaned any money to Don Richards," Malone said, "that'd be a personal matter between Don Richards and me. Are you sure you won't have something to drink? Perhaps some freshly squeezed juice? What about your friend? He looks thirsty."

Kane ignored the man's second offer of a drink and said, "So, you *do* acknowledge making a loan to Mr. Richards?"

"I acknowledged nothing of the sort," Malone said with a sly, telling grin.

"Okay," Kane said reading Malone's expression, "let's suppose, *hypothetically*, that you loaned a large sum of money to Don Richards. Hypothetically, why would you loan out an amount that large to someone you'd never met or heard of?"

"Well, hypothetically, mind you," Malone said playing along, "I probably would've made use of that wonderful thing they call the internet. And while making use of said internet, I might've learned that Don Richards was a highly successful businessman who was both dependable and wealthy. That might have given me the incentive I needed to make the loan—at a very high-interest rate, of course."

"Of course," Kane said. "And if you were to make such a loan, what would the terms of the loan be in relation to when the loan should be paid off. How long would Mr. Richards have before he was in arrears of the debt?"

While Kane and Malone talked, Earl marveled at his friend's skill. "No wonder he was such a successful corporate negotiator," he thought to himself.

"Why, Mr. Kane," Malone said, "any man in my position would be a fool if he were to make an excessively large loan to someone and then allow that individual to leave town before he'd paid the loan in full."

Earl's eyes widened.

"So, if you'd made such a loan," Kane said, "your debtor would be in arrears if he left town before he'd paid the loan in full?"

"Do I come across to you as being a fool, Mr. Kane?" Malone asked.

"No, you don't," Kane said gravely.

"Then you have your answer," Malone said with a serious look on his face—his first serious look since the conversation began.

Kane asked, "And what is your follow-up procedure with someone who leaves town without first clearing their debt with you?"

"Mr. Kane," Malone said looking thoughtful, "any good financial institution takes various steps to provide their debtors with the necessary incentive to pay their debt. They'll send letters, make phone calls, send emails, and such like. In these letters and phones calls, they'll often make certain threats.

They'll threaten to repossess or foreclose, or they may threaten to file a lawsuit or to turn them over to a collection agency. Threats can be very effective, Mr. Kane."

"And you operate in the same fashion as these financial institutions you mentioned?"

"I do."

"You make threats?"

"I do."

"And what is the nature of the threats you make, Mr. Malone?"

Ollie Malone's face went stoic in response to Kane's question. He stood silently and considered Kane for a few moments. Then he turned and spoke to the two large men who'd escorted Kane and Earl up to the penthouse, "Gentleman, my new friends here are anxious to get out and tour our lovely city. Would you please see them safely to the entrance of the building?"

"Yes, sir," one of the men said as they made their way toward where Kane and Earl stood.

Earl tensed himself up in preparation for an old-fashioned Tennessee tangle right there in the penthouse of a fancy Las Vegas hotel/casino. The men stopped just before they reached them. One of them motioned gracefully with his arm toward the hallway from where they'd entered a few minutes earlier. Kane took the lead and walked briskly and professionally toward the elevators. Their meeting with Mr. Ollie Malone was over.

Kane and Earl were hungry after they left the casino. They stopped in at a nearby café to eat and discuss their meeting with Malone. They also discussed what their next step would be.

Earl noticed a well-dressed man sitting in a corner booth while they ate. The man appeared to be in his mid-twenties. His suit was nice, but not fancy. Earl saw the man glance in their direction several times. It could've been Earl's overalls and black tee-shirt that drew the man's attention, but Earl didn't think so. The man followed them when they left the restaurant. Earl noticed. Not only was the man following them, he evidently wasn't too concerned about being inconspicuous.

"Let's walk down the strip this way and see if we can pick up some more information," Kane said. "Our flight isn't until six thirty-five. We may as well make good use of our time while we're here."

They visited two more nearby casinos without learning anything helpful. Folks weren't willing to talk. Not about the things Kane and Earl wanted to discuss anyway. The very mention of Malone's name made folks scurry away politely with anxiety in their eyes. When they left the second casino Earl saw the man who'd been tailing them. He decided to mention it to Kane.

"I'm pretty sure somebody's following us, Cuz. I kind of expected it though."

"Yes, I've noticed our new friend as well," Kane said. "Let's walk this way. I see a clearing between those two casinos there. Let's see if he follows along."

Before they started walking, a black limousine with heavily tinted windows pulled up alongside the strange man. A back window rolled down, and an arm handed the man a legal-sized manila envelope.

"I wonder what that could be," Earl said.

"Come on. Let's go," Kane said as he turned and walked swiftly in the direction he indicated earlier. They walked several yards and stopped on the sidewalk just in front of an empty lot with a large sign that advertised a new hotel/casino. They turned around to look for the man who was tailing them. He wasn't there. Kane looked across the street. He saw a couple of tall buildings beyond the sidewalk. The streets weren't overly crowded, but several people were walking down the sidewalk on the other side. Earl looked behind them a few moments later and saw the man again. He was walking briskly toward them. Earl tensed up in preparation to defend them against an attack when he felt Kane's hand on his shoulder.

"He doesn't look armed, Earl. Besides, he only has one free hand because of that envelope he's carrying. To top it all off, he's half your size. Let's play it cool and see what he wants."

When the man reached them, he handed the envelope to Kane and said, "Compliments of Mr. Ollie Malone."

"Oh?" Kane said, "What is it?"

The man gestured for Kane to open the envelope, "Be my guest."

Kane pulled the contents out of the envelope and looked them over. He said to Earl, "They're airlines tickets. Two flights from Paradise to Nashville scheduled to leave at one thirty-five this afternoon."

Earl looked at the man and said with a hint of irritation, "We've already got tickets for a flight back to Nashville. We're scheduled to leave at six thirty-five. I think we'll just wait and take that flight."

The man turned and pointed to the large sign that stood directly behind Kane and Earl. Kane and Earl turned and saw a bullet hole in the center of one of the Os in "Coming Soon."

"What in the world?" Earl said. They turned back around, and the man was holding a pair of binoculars in his extended hand. Earl took the binoculars and looked through them toward the top of a tall building across the street the man indicated. He saw a man on top of the roof with a rifle trained directly on them. Earl handed the binoculars to Kane.

Kane looked through the binoculars and focused on the shooter. He handed the binoculars back to the man, looked at Earl, and said, "I think I've learned everything I need to know. Let's make our way to the airport and take the flight our friend Mr. Malone has graciously arranged for us."

Earl and Kane were sitting in the airplane on the runway awaiting takeoff. Earl turned to Kane and said, "I guess you *have* learned everything you need to know, Cuz. That conversation with Malone about making threats was very telling. It was particularly interesting how Malone reacted when you asked him about the nature of the threats he makes toward his debtors. And it's clear that Malone has highly skilled snipers at his disposal. That certainly makes Malone a good suspect in this murder investigation."

Kane shifted around in his seat until he got comfortable. He opened the book he'd selected to read during the flight home. Just before losing himself in the book, he said, “On the contrary, Earl, seeing the sniper on top of that building confirmed without question that Ollie Malone had absolutely nothing to do with Linda Richards’ murder.”

TWENTY-THREE

KANE ARRIVED AT HIS office at his usual time on Friday morning. Leann arrived ahead of him again—coffee ready.

"Good morning," Kane said.

"Good morning, how'd your trip go? Anything promising?" Leann said.

"It turned out to be a dead-end, but that's a good thing. It frees us up so we can devote our full attention to our most likely suspect—Johnny Ray."

"Why was it a dead-end? Weren't you able to visit the loan shark?"

"Oh yes, we visited him alright."

Kane gave her the details of his and Earl's trip to Vegas.

"They shot at you?" Leann said.

"They shot in our direction. If they'd wanted to shoot us they could've very well accomplished it. They just wanted to warn us."

"But doesn't all this suggest that they could be

the ones who murdered Linda Richards?"

"That's what Earl thought too," Kane said. "But if you consider the facts, you can see why I think it actually proves they're *not* guilty of murdering Linda Richards. If Ollie Malone wanted to assassinate Linda Richards to issue a strong warning to Don Richards that he needs to pay his debt, he could've simply sent a hit-man down to do the job. The hit-man would've been unknown to anyone in Middle Tennessee, and he would've worked discreetly. So why would the hit-man bother with an elaborate scheme to frame someone for the murder? He wouldn't care anything about that. He'd just sneak into town, assassinate his victim, and sneak out again."

Kane poured a cup of coffee and stirred in some cream and sweetener, "When Ollie sent that man to shoot at us in broad daylight on the strip in Vegas, he made it clear that he's willing to kill, if necessary. He's probably done so in the past. But it also made me realize that his hit-men are willing to take risks by shooting at someone on a busy street in broad daylight. It'd be nothing to them to shoot a woman on a lonely street in Middle Tennessee in the early morning hours. So again, why would they bother framing someone for it? And it's clear that somebody went to a great deal of trouble to frame Jeremy for this murder."

"Yes," Leann said. "I see what you mean."

"What about the funeral?" she asked Kane.

"I assume you're referring to Linda Richards' funeral," Kane said. "I saw that they scheduled the service for today at two o'clock, but we won't be going."

"None of us?"

"None of us," Kane answered. "I'm sympathetic about the great loss Don Richards and others have suffered in Linda Richards' death. But it wouldn't comfort them in the least if we showed up at the funeral. It'd probably have the opposite effect. Remember, we're the enemy as far as Don Richards' is concerned. We're defending the man accused of murdering his wife. I'm confident that he agrees with that accusation. If he saw us there, it'd only upset him and his friends and family that much more."

"You're right, of course. I guess I hadn't thought about it from that perspective."

"We haven't been able to speak to Don Richards personally for the same reasons. We've had to rely on other sources to gather information about him."

"What do you think about him in light of what we've learned so far?" Leann asked.

While they'd been talking, Kane had opened the file that contained the pictures Leann took at the crime scene and was flipping through them again.

"Something keeps gnawing at me about some of these pictures," he said. "Especially those you took of the shower stall."

"What's wrong with them?" Leann asked.

"I don't know. I can't put my finger on anything specific. But something seems out of place. I'm sorry, what did you ask me?"

"Huh? Oh, yes, I asked what you thought about Don Richards in light of everything we've learned so far."

"Well, we only have a few pieces—certainly not the whole picture. The picture we *can* construct out of what we know seems to be alright. Nothing stands out against him except his recent gambling tryst, of course. That could very well bring him to financial ruin. But it seems like he's doing everything he can to pay off those debts as quickly as possible."

"Do you think we should look into him further?" Leann asked.

"It may eventually come to that," Kane said. "But it'll have to be later on down the road. We don't have time for a thorough investigation into him before the preliminary hearing on Monday. So far, there's nothing to implicate him in the murder of his wife. I believe we're justified in pursuing Johnny Ray. If we can't get the charges against Jeremy dismissed at the preliminary hearing, we'll probably look further into Don Richards if the Johnny Ray lead fizzles out. But that lead looks mighty strong right now. Our job is to get the charges dropped against Jeremy. If we find a more likely suspect, it'll go a long way toward accomplishing that. After we get those charges dropped, it'll be the DA's job to find out who the real killer is."

"Are you sure you can get those charges dropped at the hearing? If the judge sends Jeremy's case to the Supreme Court, it'll just add more validity to the prosecutor's case. And bail probably won't be granted because of the nature of the charges. Jeremy could sit in jail for a long time before the actual trial."

Kane said, "Bowling has some pretty compelling evidence against Jeremy. As I said, our only real hope is to find someone more likely to be the killer. Johnny Ray is a good prospect, but we've got to prove he did it. We're also limited to what we can introduce at the hearing. Remember, a preliminary hearing is mostly the prosecutor's show. Its entire purpose is to test the prosecutor's charges against the accused. But thankfully Judge Newman will be presiding."

"That's a good thing?" Leann asked.

"About as good as we can hope for," Kane said. "Judge Newman is a fair man. He truly wants to see justice done. And, like us, he's sensitive to the fact that there're several people behind bars for crimes they didn't commit. He's also an old family friend. He knew my father and my grandfather and respected both of them. He'll usually allow me more leeway than is normally allowed a defense attorney at a preliminary hearing in cross-examining the witnesses and scrutinizing the evidence introduced by the prosecution."

The door buzzer rang out front. Leann stepped out of Kane's office to see who it was. She reentered his office moments later with Earl by her side. Kane was still sitting at his desk poring over the pictures of the crime scene.

Earl held up a small card between his fingers, "Here it is." He handed the card to Kane who examined it thoroughly.

"It's well-done—looks very professional," Kane said.

"What is it?" Leann asked.

"It's my business card apparently," Kane said.

"But you don't use business cards."

"No, I don't. I never have. Remember when Jeremy told us about the man who visited him at his workplace early Tuesday morning just before he clocked out?"

"Yes, I remember. The man struck up a conversation about local celebrities. He mentioned you."

"That's right," Kane said. "Jeremy and I discussed that man again. Jeremy told me the man gave him one of my business cards. I told Earl to swing by the Hensley's house this morning and get it from Jeremy's car."

"But why would someone do such a thing?" Leann asked.

"It's my theory that someone wanted Jeremy to think to come to my office shortly after he found the abduction note on the morning the murder took place. They wanted him in the house up to a certain point in time after the shooting, but then they needed him to get out of the house so they could return Jeremy's shoes and hide the rifle under the Hensley's house before Roger arrived. They didn't want him going to the police, and they warned him about that in the note they left. So, they planted the seed in his head about me hoping he'd leave the house and go straight to my office."

"That's a pretty good theory, Cuz," Earl said.

Kane continued, "I can't think of any other reason why someone would show up out of the blue on that particular morning to give Jeremy one of my business cards—especially since I don't use business cards. Someone obviously made up those cards on their computer and gave one to this mysterious man to give to Jeremy."

"They could've easily gotten all the information they needed for the card from those websites about you," Leann said.

"Yes, whoever's responsible for Linda Richards' death has made a lot of use of the internet in framing Jeremy for this murder," Kane said thoughtfully.

"Earl," Kane said. "Johnny Ray told me he was eating breakfast at a restaurant on the other side of Murfreesboro during the time of Linda Richards' murder. I made some phone calls. He wasn't at that restaurant at all on Tuesday. You told me somebody saw his truck at a country store near Heavenly Way on Tuesday morning between six thirty and seven o'clock. I want you to dig up some more information about that. See if you can confirm that his truck was there. And see if you can find out what time he parked it there, and what time he left."

"*If* I can?" Earl smiled.

"Thanks, Earl. I appreciate it."

Earl was about to open Kane's office door to leave when Leann said to Kane, "Well, you know? It's lunchtime, and I'm getting hungry, you know. Should I have something delivered here or should we go out and eat, you know?"

Earl stopped and shut the door. He turned to Kane and said, "What's she doing?"

"Oh, she's just mimicking Johnny Ray. She was somewhat irritated by the way he spoke when we interviewed him. He kept adding 'you know' to everything he said."

Earl could hardly contain his excitement. "Didn't you read my notes on my interview with Rabbit?" He asked.

"I'm sorry. I didn't," Kane said. "I've read all your other notes from the other interviews, but after our discussion about your talk with Rabbit, I was certain the only significant thing you'd gotten from him was that somebody purchased an M107 sniper rifle under shady circumstances. Why?"

Earl said, "Rabbit started going into his craziness at the end of the interview. He blurted out 'you know' over and over again. He even sang it to random tunes. I thought it was just his usual nuttiness, but when I asked him about it, he said the man who bought the rifle from Bruce kept saying 'you know' after everything he said."

Leann's eyes brightened. She said, "You've got to be kidding. That seals it! Johnny Ray has *got* to be the murderer."

Kane sat silent for a few moments to let the new information sink in.

"What do you think, Cuz?" Earl asked. "With everything else we know about ole Johnny Ray, this certainly does seem to drive the last nail in the coffin for him."

"Yes, it certainly *seems* that way," Kane said. "Earl, it's more urgent now than ever for you to get me the information I just asked you to get."

Earl walked through the door and shot back over his shoulder, "I'm on it, Cuz."

TWENTY-FOUR

IT WAS TWENTY MINUTES past eight o'clock on Monday morning. Kane and Leann were sitting in Kane's office drinking coffee and waiting anxiously to hear from Earl. They had to leave for Murfreesboro by 8:30 to make it to the preliminary hearing on time. At 8:22, Earl rushed through the front door of the outer office and went straight into Kane's office in the back.

"You're not going to believe this, Cuz." He said.

"Where've you been, Earl?" Kane said. "Why didn't you call or text by now? We've got to be leaving for the courthouse."

"I'm sorry, Kane. My phone's not getting any signal this morning for some reason. Anyway, Johnny Ray is off the hook."

"What?" Leann exclaimed.

"He's got a rock-solid alibi," Earl said.

Kane grabbed his briefcase and headed for the door, "Come on you two. We can discuss it on the way to Murfreesboro. We'll go in my truck."

They got settled quickly into Kane's truck and headed toward Murfreesboro. Kane said, "Okay, Earl. What's the story?"

"Well, I wasn't able to track down anybody at that country store all weekend. A sign said they'd closed the store due to the flu. It turns out that the owner and his wife run the store themselves. They've got a girl who works for a couple of hours in the evenings. Besides that, they don't have any other employees except for a man who helps them cook breakfast in the back. He comes in at five o'clock in the morning and works until nine o'clock in the morning. I finally caught the owners at the store this morning. They didn't open until seven thirty because they'd both been down with the flu all weekend."

"What'd they have to say? Did they know anything about Johnny Ray's truck being parked in their parking lot last Tuesday morning?"

"Oh yes, Cuz. They know quite a bit about Johnny Ray as a matter of fact. He works for them at the store."

Leann's eyes widened, "he works for them?"

"That's right. He's the man who cooks for them from five o'clock until nine o'clock in the morning. In fact, he was there from five to nine last Tuesday morning when somebody killed Linda Richards."

"He never left. Not even for a break?" Leann asked.

"That would have to be a long break. He'd have to walk fifteen minutes through the woods, shoot Linda Richards, plant the evidence to frame Jeremy, and then walk another fifteen minutes back to the store. But that's all irrelevant anyway. Both the owner and his wife insisted that Johnny never left the store that morning. And it's a small store. They would've noticed if he'd left."

"But why would Johnny lie to us about where he was that morning?" Leann asked.

"I asked the owner about that," Earl said. "He said Johnny asked him not to tell anyone about it when he hired him. The factory where Johnny works frowns on moonlighting. But Johnny's wife lost her job and wasn't able to find another one. Johnny didn't have a choice. They needed the money. He probably lied to you because he was trying to keep his employment at the country store a secret so he could protect his main job at the factory."

Leann was frustrated. She kept asking questions as if she could change the obvious fact that Johnny Ray was at the store in front of two witnesses on the morning of the murder. "But what about all the other evidence? What about the fact that he says 'you know' after all his sentences. The man who bought the rifle from Bruce did the same thing."

Earl shrugged, "There has to be another explanation. It was probably a coincidence."

"I can't believe this," Leann said. "Everything was hanging on Johnny Ray being the real killer. Now we're back to square one. And here we are driving to the courthouse for the preliminary hearing. We'll be walking into that courtroom empty-handed."

Kane was listening quietly to the conversation

while he drove. He was trying to think of any other possible options. Something was still bothering him. He just couldn't put his finger on it. Those pictures! Something Leann said back at the Richards' house on the morning of the murder. What was it? He had asked her about it, but she couldn't remember. He could only hope it'd come to him in the next few minutes. Jeremy's freedom depended on it.

TWENTY-FIVE

KANE WANTED TO PAUSE and admire the historic beauty of the courthouse. But time was short. Having Judge Dean Newman preside over Jeremy's preliminary hearing was an advantage. But the judge had no tolerance for tardiness. Kane parked his truck, and they rushed into the courthouse and entered the stately courtroom.

Kane and Leann got settled behind the defense table in the imposing dark-paneled courtroom. Kane laid out the contents of his briefcase, fired up his laptop, and started looking around the room. He'd never seen such a display at a preliminary hearing before. Bowling wasn't leaving anything to chance. He was pulling out all the stops to make sure Jeremy's case went to trial.

The witnesses were filing into the courtroom—a lot of them. Bowling even had the glass shower stall removed intact from the Richards' deck and placed inside the courtroom. Kane shook his head when he thought about the tremendous efforts that must've gone into in such a project.

Prosecutors weren't required to offer discovery that early in the criminal process in the state of Tennessee. Many prosecutors were careful not to give away too much at the preliminary hearing. The same was true for defense attorneys. If they revealed too much during the preliminary hearing, they'd be offering the other side an opportunity to prepare themselves to handle such should the case be bound over to the Supreme Court.

The prosecutor's burden at a preliminary hearing was two-fold. First, he had to prove a crime had been committed. Then he had to demonstrate probable cause that the accused had committed the crime. The prosecutor could usually convince the judge without having to lay out the entire case before him.

But Bowling wasn't taking any chances with Jeremy's case. He was up against Tyler Kane. Even though more than ninety percent of cases that go through the preliminary hearing process end up going to trial, Kane was known for getting his clients' charges dismissed at the hearings. Bowling also had the DA breathing down his neck because he didn't want to be publicly humiliated by Kane again. Bowling clearly intended to bring out all of his guns—even the big guns. He wanted his argument to be a slam dunk so he could walk out of the courtroom a victor—ready to show off for the news cameras. And Bowling had some mighty big guns to use against Jeremy from everything Kane had learned. Most preliminary hearings lasted anywhere from thirty minutes to two hours. But it was clear that Bowling intended to drag this one out all day long if necessary.

Now that Kane was able to see the shower stall again in real time, he began to wonder again what he was missing. "Oh well," he thought to himself. "Whatever it is, I'm just not seeing it."

Kane turned around and gazed across the courtroom toward the entrance doors. The courtroom was filling up fast. The news of Linda Richards' murder wasn't insignificant. People were interested. He watched as Earl helped a thin, attractive, middle-aged woman down the aisle and into a seat. He figured it was Jeremy's mother. He felt ashamed that he hadn't had a chance to visit with her before the hearing.

Kane looked across the aisle and saw Bowling standing at the prosecutor's table flipping through a file. He was talking quietly with his assistant. Bowling looked over, caught Kane's eye, and gave him a smug wink. Kane held Bowling's gaze for a moment then turned back to face the front of the courtroom.

A court officer entered the courtroom a couple of minutes later and called for everyone to stand, "The honorable Judge Dean Newman presiding."

Jeremy was escorted into the room through a side door and then to the defendant's table. He didn't look well, but he looked as good as any college student would whose busy life had been interrupted by an accusation of murder.

Kane studied Judge Newman and tried to gauge his mood. The judge didn't look particularly well.

His skin was flush, and small beads of sweat dotted his forehead. It could bode badly for Jeremy if the judge didn't feel well. With the weight of evidence Bowling had at his disposal, Judge Newman could very well cut the hearing short and turn Jeremy's case over to trial.

"I don't have much to offer anyway," Kane thought to himself. They'd done as much investigating as they could in the limited amount of time they had. They made some significant discoveries about Johnny Ray, but that lead fell flat at the last minute. Leann was right. They had practically nothing to offer in Jeremy's defense. Kane had a couple of cards up his sleeve, but he knew it wouldn't be enough. All he could do was hope Bowling would make a mistake—A big one. But that wasn't likely.

Kane saw Bowling in action on the basketball court, the football field, and the wrestling mat when they were younger. But he'd never seen him in action in the courtroom. He was about to learn that Bowling's impressive skills weren't limited to sports.

TWENTY-SIX

BOWLING DIDN'T WASTE ANY time establishing that a crime had been committed. Sheriff Brown's testimony along with that of a couple of other witnesses confirmed that Linda Richards died from a single gunshot wound to the heart. Death could've occurred anytime between five and eight o'clock the previous Tuesday morning according to the coroner.

The shot was fired sometime just after seven o'clock according to Don Richard's testimony. To top it off, Bowling called in a technical expert to explain how the accelerometer in Linda Richards' fitness watch worked. The expert explained how they used the accelerometer to determine the exact time she fell after being shot. It removed all doubt as to the exact time of death—7:05 a.m. Kane had nothing to add and no questions to ask during that phase of the procedure. Somebody murdered Linda Richard's, and no one disputed it.

It was time for Bowling's real show. He had the burden of demonstrating probable cause that Jeremy Scott committed the murder. But it was hardly a burden given the available evidence. He called Larry Clemmons to the stand as his first witness. Larry Clemmons was a detective who helped investigate the crime scene.

"Mr. Clemmons," Bowling began, "We've established that the victim died as a result of a gunshot wound through the heart. Can you tell us the location from which the shot was fired?"

"The shooter made the shot from a tree about eighty-three yards out in a field that lies between the Richards' house and another house owned by a man and his wife by the name of Hensley."

"How can you be certain that the shooter fired from that particular spot?"

"We found fresh sole imprints in the soft dirt around the tree. There were also several scuff marks on the tree where the shooter broke off some bark while he climbed the tree."

Bowling held up a black strap about ten feet long, "Was this also found in the tree?"

"Yes, sir."

"And what is it?"

"We believe it's a strap the shooter used to steady his rifle while he made the shot. It was found hanging on another branch directly above the branch we believe the shooter crouched on when he fired the shot."

"How can you be sure what branch he crouched on to fire the shot?"

"Being crouched on that branch would place him

in a spot where he was perfectly level with the height of the bullet holes we found in the glass panels of the shower stall."

"You mentioned finding some sole imprints in the soft dirt around the tree where the shooter fired the shot. Have you been able to identify these soles?"

"We found a pair of running shoes in the Hensley's house where the defendant was staying. We confirmed that the shoes belong to the defendant. The soles of the shoes were a perfect match when we compared them to the imprints we found around the tree."

"Did you find any imprints anywhere else that matched these shoes?"

"Yes, sir. We found partial imprints underneath the Hensley's House."

"What else did you find underneath the house?"

"The imprints along with some scuff marks led us to the front part of the house where we noticed some loose dirt. We found an M107 sniper rifle buried in that spot about one foot underground."

Bowling asked a few more routine questions before he called his next witness. Kane had nothing to ask detective Clemmons at that time.

Bowling's next witness was the forensics expert who handled all the evidence for the case. After the expert was duly sworn in, Bowling held up Jeremy's running shoes and asked,

"Have you examined the imprints along with the soles on the bottom of these running shoes?"

"Yes, sir. I have."

"And what is your conclusion?"

"It's my conclusion that the soles on those shoes match perfectly with the imprints found in the soft soil around the tree where the shooter fired the deadly shot. They also match the partial imprints found under the Hensley's house."

Kane thought he'd be able to get a slight jab in with the forensics expert. He'd show how that particular style of shoe was highly popular. Then he'd point out the likelihood that hundreds and perhaps even thousands of people all over the county owned shoes exactly like those. It wasn't much, but that's what he planned to ask until Bowling displayed his abilities with his next question.

"There must be thousands of people who own shoes identical to these. Did you find anything that can positively connect Jeremy's shoes to the imprints found in the soil around the tree and underneath the house?"

"Yes, sir. I examined samples of the soil from underneath the tree and of the soil from underneath the Hensley's house. The two soils differ significantly in type. But I found particles of both types of soil embedded in the soles of the defendant's shoes."

Kane looked particularly frustrated. "What is it?" Leann asked.

"Bowling is good. On top of that, he's got a mountain of evidence to be good with. I don't see how we can keep this thing from going to trial."

Bowling continued his questioning. "Detective Clemmons mentioned a rifle they'd found buried underneath the Hensley's house. Can you confirm the rifle's type?"

"Yes, sir. It was an M107 sniper rifle."

"And tests revealed that this was, in fact, the rifle used to murder Linda Richards?"

"Conclusively."

"Other than the fact that they found the rifle underneath the Hensley's house where the defendant was staying, is there anything else that would connect the rifle to the defendant?"

"Yes, sir. We found a fingerprint on the front part of the trigger guard. I've positively identified that fingerprint as belonging to the defendant."

"There were no other fingerprints found on the gun anywhere?"

"No, sir. The gun had been wiped clean."

"If the gun had been wiped clean, how can you explain the fact that there was one fingerprint on the gun?" Bowling asked.

The witness answered, "Shooters often rest their finger on the front part of the trigger guard while they're waiting for their target to come into view. They often do this subconsciously. They usually remember to wipe off the trigger, but they forget about the trigger guard."

"I have in the courtroom a glass shower stall. Can you identify this stall?" Bowling asked the forensics expert.

"Yes, sir. It has my tag on it. That's the stall Linda Richards was standing in front of when the bullet entered her body."

"Did you have the opportunity to investigate the crime scene before we moved the stall?"

"Yes, sir. I did."

"Very well. Is there a way to verify the direction from which the bullet came?"

Sound evidence had already demonstrated that the bullet came from a tree located in the field that lay between the Richards' house and the Hensley's house. But Bowling wanted to drive the point home and leave no doubt. He wanted the judge to fully understand that the shot was fired from a place that was quickly and easily accessible to Jeremy.

"Yes, sir. There is."

"Could you explain it to us please?"

The forensics expert got up from his seat and walked over to the shower stall. "This is the back panel of the stall," he began. "It was on the edge of the south side of the deck. When you examine the hole where the bullet passed through it, you can see that the glass is flat where the bullet entered. On the other side of this panel, you can see that the bullet hole is spread out slightly. So the bullet exited from this side of the panel inside the stall. We can observe the same thing from the other bullet hole in the front panel of the stall. There's no question about it. The shooter fired the bullet from the south side of the back panel of the stall, and the tree from which he fired lies south of the Richards' house. The Hensley's house lies just south of the tree."

Kane sat up with a start while the witness gave his explanation. Leann noticed.

"What is it?" she asked. "Did you think of something?"

Kane suddenly realized what he'd been trying to see in those pictures. The way the shower stall sat in the courtroom put it in the direct sunlight that shone through a side window. He saw it. It was as plain as day. He remembered what Leann said at the crime scene. A hundred details rushed through his mind and connected—details from conversations with various people, seemingly insignificant details from Earl's notes of his interview with Jeremy's mom, and from other interviews. Things that on the face had no significance became very significant. Things that had no connection whatsoever suddenly connected perfectly. He had the answer. He knew who murdered Linda Richards. And he knew exactly how the killer did it!

But he saw it too late. He couldn't offer one piece of anything tangible to demonstrate that what he saw would exonerate Jeremy. "Wait a minute. There's one way to prove it," he thought to himself. "But there's no way I can get to it in time."

He slumped back in his chair frustrated. "If we could only get a recess. But that's unheard of during a preliminary hearing. But wait," he continued to reason. "Bowling obviously plans to drag this thing out. Maybe there is a chance."

Kane turned around and got Earl's attention. He whispered detailed instructions to him. He handed Earl the keys to his truck when he finished and said, "Please hurry, Earl. Jeremy's freedom depends on this."

Earl rose from his seat and walked over to Jeremy's mom. He had a brief exchange with her, then he walked over to Sheriff Brown's seat and whispered in his ear. The sheriff got up and accompanied Earl out of the courtroom.

"Mr. Kane," Judge Newman repeated irritably,

"do you have any questions for this witness?"

"Pardon me, Your Honor. Yes, I have one question."

Kane didn't have any meaningful questions to ask the witness. But if he didn't get involved soon, the Judge would bring the hearing to a halt and declare that there was sufficient evidence to bind Jeremy's case over to the Grand Jury. And Kane had definitely found a reason to encourage Bowling to drag the thing out.

Kane asked the witness, "Besides the one fingerprint found on the trigger guard, were there any other identifying marks that connect the rifle with the defendant? For example, were there any identification numbers on the gun?"

"No, sir. Someone filed all identifying marks including any numbers off of the gun."

"So, there's no other way to trace the gun back to any specific owner? The defendant for example?"

"No, sir."

"Thank you. No further questions at this time, Your Honor."

Bowling called Rufus Swartz to the stand—a gun expert who specialized in sniper rifles. He went through the process of testing Mr. Swartz' credentials, then he asked, "Mr. Swartz, are you familiar with the M107 Sniper rifle?"

"Yes, sir, very familiar."

"Very well. Is an M107 sniper rifle capable of making this accurate of a shot from a distance of eighty-three yards?"

"In the right hands, that rifle is capable of making such a shot from one hundred yards away.

Possibly more, if the shooter is highly skilled."

"So, your answer to the question is 'yes'?"

"My answer is yes."

"No further questions, Your Honor."

"Cross?" the Judge asked.

"No, Your Honor," Kane said.

Kane was pleased when Bowling called his next witness. Tim Johns was a handwriting expert who'd made a career out of testifying in court. He was good at what he did, and he was articulate on the stand. Kane knew that with the evidence Bowling had presented, coupled with the fact that Judge Newman didn't feel well, the judge was likely to call this thing off and bind Jeremy's case over to the Grand Jury at any moment. Kane didn't have much ammunition, but he had a little he could bring out with Tim Johns—ammunition that might stall the judge's decision until Earl could complete his mission with the sheriff.

Bowling verified the witness's credentials and began the questioning, "Mr. Johns, do you recognize this letter?" Bowling held up the abduction note Jeremy claimed to find on the Hensley's nightstand on the morning of the murder.

"Yes, sir. It has my mark on it."

"Have you examined this letter along with a sample of the defendant's handwriting?"

"Yes, sir. I have."

"And have you concluded that the handwriting in this letter is identical with that of the defendant's?"

"Yes, sir. There's no question about it. The handwriting in that letter is identical to the defendant's handwriting."

"So, there's no question that the defendant wrote that abduction note himself?'

Kane sprang from his seat, "Objection, Your Honor. Supposition."

"Sustained. Please rephrase the question," the judge said to Bowling. Bowling paced in a small circle for a few moments searching for how to ask his question in a way that would get him the results he desired. He finally looked satisfied and said,

"Mr. Johns, would you say this style of cursive is unique?"

"Yes, sir. I'd say it's extremely unique. In all of my years studying handwriting, I've never seen anything quite like it."

Bowling smiled. He was pleased with the answer along with the implication attached to it.

"Thank you," Bowling said. "I have no further questions."

"Cross?" the Judge asked.

"Yes sir, Your Honor." Kane noticed again how bad the Judge looked. His sweating had intensified, and he seemed to be shifting around in his seat more and more.

"Mr. Johns," Kane began, "you've testified that the writing in the abduction note is identical with samples of the defendant's handwriting and that there's no question about it."

"That's correct."

"You also affirmed that it's a unique style of handwriting and in all of your years of experience in these matters you've never seen anything like it?"

"That's right. Never."

Kane pulled another letter out of his pocket and

said, “Mr. Johns, would you please examine this letter for me.” Kane made the proper motion to enter the letter into evidence and then handed it to Mr. Johns along with the abduction letter.

Mr. Johns looked at the letter closely for a few moments and said, “Why it’s just a copy of the abduction letter.”

“What’s written on the bottom of the letter you claim is a copy?”

“There’s a signature there. I believe it says ‘Leann Walker’.”

“And what’s written above that signature?”

“It says, ‘I affirm that I, Leann Walker, wrote the above letter with my own hand.’”

“And what’s below Miss Walker’s signature?”

“The name and signature of another woman. She affirmed that she witnessed Miss Walker write the above note. She also notarized it.”

Kane walked over to his table and picked up a clicker. He pressed a button, and the screen of his laptop computer was projected onto a large screen a court officer set up in the courtroom the previous evening at Kane’s request.

“What do you see on the screen, Mr. Johns?” Kane asked.

“It looks like a website of some sort.”

“What about the writing, Mr. Johns? What you’re seeing is the defendant’s blog. He’s been running this blog for four years. He writes poetry out on paper and then photographs what he wrote and posts it on his blog.”

“Objection, Your Honor,” Bowling said. He spread his arms out and added, “This is all so pointless. We already have samples of the defendant's handwriting."

"If you'll allow me a couple of moments, Your Honor. I'll show the relevance."

The judge rubbed his chin thoughtfully. Then he shifted uncomfortably in his seat and said, "I'll allow it, but make it quick. Overruled."

"As I said," Kane continued hurriedly, "what you're seeing is a blog the defendant has run for four years. The blog has hundreds of poems—all written in the defendant's unique cursive hand."

Kane pressed the button on the clicker to advance to the next slide. The slide displayed a more technical page with graphs and numbers.

Kane said, "Only the administrator of the site can view this particular page. I'm displaying it now with the defendant's permission. It gives the details about the activity of the website. You can see how many views he's had, what's been viewed the most, and so forth. Most significantly, you can see the geographic area from which the views are coming. Notice that the defendant has more than one thousand followers from the Middle Tennessee area alone. Mr. Johns has already verified that my assistant, Leann Walker, can mimic the defendant's handwriting. And she did it in a way that fooled Mr. Johns himself. And he's an expert in such matters. He actually thought Miss Walker's note was an exact copy of the abduction letter. Any of the defendant's thousands of followers could've done the same thing if they wanted to make someone think that Jeremy wrote that abduction note himself."

"Thank you. I have no further questions, Your Honor," Kane said as he walked back to his table.

"That was amazing!" Leann said. "I had no idea why you wanted me to write that letter. You should've seen Bowling's face when you made that last point."

Kane shook his head, "It's not much, but it helps. It'll at least buy us some time."

The judge suddenly rose to his feet. That was odd. He addressed Bowling, "Mr. Bowling, I haven't decided on this matter yet. And it looks like I'll need to hear more before I make my decision. Do you have more to introduce?"

"Yes, Your Honor," Bowling said disappointed that the Judge hadn't yet concluded that Jeremy's case needed to go to trial.

"Very well," the Judge continued. "It's eleven o'clock. I'm going to call a two-hour recess. We'll reconvene here at one o'clock." The Judge brought down his gavel, turned, and quickly exited the courtroom.

Kane was shocked, but he wasn't complaining. It was exactly what he needed. He had something he needed to do. He wasn't sure if two hours would be enough time, but he had to try.

"Leann, we need to get to Smyrna as fast as we can. We don't have a minute to lose."

"I'm afraid we're going to have to lose a couple of minutes," she said.

"What do you mean?"

"We'll have to take a minute to find some transportation. Earl took your truck."

TWENTY-SEVEN

KANE BRUSHED PAST LEANN and rushed out of the courtroom, “Come on.”

He scanned the parking lot trying to think of what to do. “We’ll have to call a cab,” he said.

“Wait a minute!” Leann said. “My stepmom’s real estate office is just a couple of blocks over. Let’s hurry. We can borrow her car.”

Leann sent her stepmom a text while they ran to tell her they needed to borrow her car and that she would explain later. She asked her to meet them in the parking lot with the keys.

A few minutes later they were speeding down the highway away from Murfreesboro and toward Smyrna.

“Slow down,” Kane said. “We don’t have time to get pulled over.”

“We’re almost to Smyrna. Where are we going?” Leann asked.

Kane looked at the app he’d opened for

directions, “We’re going to the home office of SWAG. I’ll turn the voice option on so you can follow the directions.”

“SWAG?”

“Yes, if you’ll remember, it’s one of the businesses Don Richards’ investment club owns. It stands for Siding, Windows, and Glass.”

“Why are we going there?”

Kane said, “If I’m right, there’re a couple of crucial pieces to this puzzle that we can only find at SWAG.”

Kane tried to text Earl a couple of times. He wasn’t getting any response. “He must be having trouble with his connection again,” Kane thought to himself. “He’s been having trouble over in that neighborhood.”

When they arrived at SWAG, Kane told Leann to wait in the car while he ran into the building. He entered the building and looked over to his right to an area where several of the company’s popular products were displayed. He was looking for something specific. He scanned the displays until his eyes rested on what he was looking for.

A young woman with glasses who looked as if she could go into labor at any moment approached him and said, “Can I help you?”

“Yes, I need to see Jim Tenry please,” Kane said. Jim Tenry was the manager of SWAG’s home office.

“He just got back from an early lunch. Can I get your name, please?”

“Tyler Kane, Attorney.”

The woman’s eyes filled with a mixture of

excitement and concern when she heard the word "attorney." She said, "One moment please."

"Thank you," Kane said. While he waited, he walked into the display section toward the product that had caught his interest.

Leann waited anxiously in the car for several minutes. She looked up and saw Kane rushing toward her with another man at his heels. Kane got into the passenger side while the other man got into the back seat.

"This is Jim Tenry," Kane said to Leann after he buckled his seatbelt. "Jim, this is my assistant Leann Walker."

Jim Tenry was a short, wiry man with muscular arms that didn't seem to fit the rest of his physique. Kane prepared him for the testimony he was about to give in the courtroom while they drove back to the courthouse.

Leann was amazed at what she heard. "Did it really happen that way?" she thought to herself. "It's incredible. Everybody's been looking at this thing from the wrong perspective from the beginning."

It occurred to Leann how significant Earl's mission was. She hoped he'd be able to find what Kane asked him to find. Without that item, Kane wouldn't be able to prove what really happened regardless of Jim Tenry's testimony.

They managed to make it back to the courthouse at about ten minutes till one despite the heavy lunch traffic. Kane scanned the parking lot for his truck and the sheriff's cruiser. He saw neither.

One of the court officers spoke to Kane when

they entered the courthouse, "The judge is feeling much better, Mr. Kane."

"What was the matter?" Kane asked.

"He was at the emergency room all night Saturday night with a bad case of food poisoning. I think he had a relapse this morning. You know how that stuff is. It gets everything all messed up. It takes a few days for your system to get up and running again."

"Yes," Kane said. He remembered getting food poisoning when he was in his teens. He wouldn't wish it on anyone, but he was still thankful for the recess.

Kane turned around again to check the entrance doors to the courtroom. It was two minutes before one o'clock. The hearing was about to resume, and there was still no sign of Earl and the sheriff. Earl still hadn't responded to any of Kane's texts.

A court officer entered the courtroom and announced the judge. It was time to begin. There was still no sign of Earl. Kane looked across the aisle at Bowling. Bowling took a couple of minor setbacks earlier, but he'd regained his air of smugness. He had every reason to be smug. All the evidence was in his favor. Kane could unravel every piece of evidence Bowling had if everything went well. But it all depended on Earl and the sheriff getting back in time with the item Kane sent them to find.

Bowling wasted no time getting his next witness

on the stand. It was Jeremy's boss from Devilish Dunkers. He was only on the stand for a couple of minutes to confirm that Jeremy had clocked out at six thirty on the morning of Linda Richards' murder. Kane had nothing to ask him. Earl had already spoken to him. He didn't know anything about the customer who'd come to speak to Jeremy that morning between six and six thirty because he was in the kitchen.

Bowling's next witness was an officer who testified that it only took about fifteen minutes to drive from Devilish Dunkers to the Hensley's house. Kane thought about how mundane it was. Bowling was being careful to establish every detail.

Bowling's next witness was a large burly man who bore a striking resemblance to Earl. The man saw Jeremy's car turning onto Heavenly Way between six thirty and seven o'clock on the morning of the murder. How in the world Bowling turned up that witness was beyond Kane. But Bowling had found him, and there was no question that Jeremy was at the Hensley's house during the time of the shooting. Kane already knew that, but Bowling made sure the judge knew it too.

The Earl lookalike stepped down from the witness box, and Bowling called Roger Johnson to the stand. After several minutes of establishing his identity and his relationship with Jeremy, Bowling simply asked him what time he'd arrived at the Hensley's house on the morning of the murder. Again, Kane had nothing to add. It was twenty minutes after one. Earl and the sheriff still hadn't made it back.

Bowling called Don Richards back to the stand. He wanted to address Jeremy's motive for killing Linda Richards.

"I understand that the defendant applied to a technical school and asked your wife to write a reference letter for him sometime back," Bowling said to Don Richards.

"That's right."

"And how would you describe the letter she wrote?"

"It was a good letter. She was honest and forthright. In my opinion the letter cast Jeremy, uh, the defendant in a good light."

"Isn't it true that your wife mentioned an incident in the letter that ultimately led to Jeremy receiving a rejection letter from the school?"

"Yes. That's true."

"What was the nature of the incident?"

"Objection," Kane said. "The details of the incident itself are not necessary to establish Mr. Bowling's point."

"Sustained." Judge Newman said.

"Okay," Bowling said. "Mr. Richards, what was Jeremy's reaction when he was denied acceptance into the school due to your wife's reference letter?"

"He was extremely upset," Don Richards said. "That school was his first choice. He was always talking about it being the school of his dreams."

"And because of your wife's reference letter, Jeremy wasn't able to attend the school of his dreams," Bowling said as more of an observation than a question. He wanted to make sure he drove the point home to show that Jeremy had a legitimate motive.

Upon cross, Kane asked Mr. Richards, "When did your wife write this reference letter?"

"I believe it was in the spring of Jeremy's senior year."

"Would March 2015 sound about right?"

"Yes. That sounds right."

"Two years ago?" Kane asked making his voice sound incredulous. "Are you suggesting that Jeremy waited around for two years before he decided to take vengeance on your wife in this extreme way?"

"Objection, Your Honor," Bowling said.

"Sustained."

"Thank you. I have nothing further, Your Honor."

Kane didn't need to explain why he'd asked what he did. It was a thin attempt to weaken the motive, but he had to try something if for no other reason than to stall for time so Earl and the sheriff could get there before everything was over. There were countless cases where murderers waited not only two years but five, ten, or twenty years before they took vengeance on someone. Bowling could easily argue that Jeremy had to wait for a suitable opportunity and that staying at the Hensley's house presented him with the opportunity he needed.

Bowling called a couple of Jeremy's friends to the stand to establish the fact that Jeremy was upset about being rejected by his dream school. Kane looked up at Judge Newman. The judge looked like he felt much better. But he also looked bored. Even worse, he looked more convinced that Jeremy could've committed the crime.

Bowling felt confident that he'd presented enough evidence to establish his case.

The judge addressed Kane, "Do you have anything to add, Mr. Kane?"

"Yes, sir," Kane said.

The moment had arrived. Earl and the sheriff weren't back yet, but Kane had no choice but to proceed. He knew he had the answer, but he couldn't prove anything until Earl got there with the evidence Kane needed.

The answer occurred to Kane earlier that morning in the courtroom. He was in the uncomfortable position of having to fly blind—something no lawyer should ever do. It would've been nice if he'd had a few weeks to investigate everything and test his conclusions. But he didn't have that luxury. He had no choice but to proceed with what he had and hope Earl arrived soon.

Kane called Jim Tenry to the stand. Tenry's testimony would be useless without the evidence he hoped Earl would find. But he had to get the ball rolling to stall the judge's decision.

"Mr. Tenry, what do you do for a living?"

"I'm the manager of SWAG out of Smyrna."

"Who owns SWAG?" Kane asked.

"It's owned by IIC, Innovative Investment Club out of Nashville."

"I see. Who's the president of this investment club?"

"That would be Mr. Don Richards."

"Mr. Don Richards, the husband of Linda Richards?"

"Yes, sir."

"Do you know Don Richards personally?"

"Yes, sir. I suppose I know him somewhat."

"Has Don Richards ever visited the home office in Smyrna where you work?"

"Yes. Many times."

Kane paced a small circle and rubbed his chin with his fingers, "How long has SWAG been in business?"

"About twenty years."

"And how long have you worked for them?"

"Almost since the beginning, seventeen years."

"And Don Richards has visited the office regularly for those seventeen years?"

"No, sir," Tenry said.

"Oh?"

"I'd never met Mr. Richards until about two weeks ago when he showed up at our main office in Smyrna."

"Was there a problem at the office?"

"Not at all."

"Then why would Don Richards, the president of the investment club, suddenly show up one day? Did you find that odd?"

"I did at first. But then he explained that he wanted to start taking more of a personal interest in the businesses they owned. He said he wanted to get more familiar with the work they do."

"Mr. Tenry, the name of your business, SWAG. That stands for Siding, Windows, and Glass, correct?"

"Yes, sir."

"What types of glass do you deal in?"

"We deal in all types of glass found in or around

a house: windows, doors, mirrors, shower stalls, and such like."

"Shower stalls. Would that include outdoor shower stalls?"

"Absolutely."

"Mr. Tenry, do you recognize the shower stall on display here in the courtroom?"

"Yes, sir. I do. That's the shower stall Mr. Richards had installed on his deck a couple of years ago."

"You can tell just by looking at it?"

"Well, no, not really. I mean, I know this hearing is about Mrs. Richards' murder. That's how I know it's their shower stall specifically. We've sold hundreds of the same model over the years. Mr. Richards had us install this one a couple of years ago."

"But I thought you hadn't met Don Richards until about two weeks ago?"

"I hadn't. He didn't come down personally to purchase the stall. He ordered it, and some of my men went out to his house to install it."

"I see," Kane said.

Kane had drug things out with Tenry long enough. Bowling was getting impatient. Kane had to keep stalling for time though. He didn't want to reveal everything with Tenry yet. He would've preferred to proceed in a different order, but he couldn't do that until Earl returned.

The entrance doors to the courtroom opened. Earl entered along with the sheriff and a couple of deputies. The sheriff was carrying a bag that contained Jeremy's M107 sniper rifle. Kane asked

Earl to bring it. Earl asked for Mrs. Scott's permission for them to enter the house and get it before he left the courtroom earlier that morning.

Earl walked down the aisle toward the front of the courtroom and gave Kane a wink. Their venture was a success.

"Your Honor," Kane said, "may I pause my questioning of this witness? I'd like to recall him to the stand later."

Judge Newman gave his approval and asked Bowling if he'd like to question the witness before he stepped down.

"If I had any clue what that was all about," Bowling said. "I wouldn't know what to ask, Your Honor."

Laughter filled the courtroom.

Kane walked over to the defense table while Jim Tenry made his way off the stand. Earl handed him a small Ziploc bag that contained the evidence Kane needed. Kane was all set, but he had to think on his feet. He wasn't sure where to begin in order to piece everything together in a way that would make sense to everyone. The things he was about to reveal would shed the entire situation in a much different light. It was imperative for him to proceed carefully.

He decided to call the gun expert back to the stand first. He'd have to ask a question he didn't know the answer to and that was risky. But the answer would set the stage for everything else he needed to reveal if it was the right answer. He proceeded with cautious confidence.

Kane asked, "Mr. Swartz, you're a gun expert who's especially adept with sniper rifles. I assume you've disassembled and reassembled several sniper rifles over the years?"

"That's correct."

"Including M107 sniper rifles?"

"Especially M107 sniper rifles."

"Mr Swartz, is it possible to remove the trigger guard from one sniper rifle and install it onto another one?"

"Absolutely. I've done it many times myself."

Kane addressed the judge and went through the proper procedure to have Jeremy's sniper rifle the sheriff had retrieved from his house entered into evidence.

"Now, Mr. Swartz, you've told us it's possible to swap out trigger guards between M107 sniper rifles. Is it possible to examine the rifles and determine whether someone had done such a thing?"

"It could be possible with two well-used rifles. But it would be difficult if both the rifles were brand new."

"Would you please examine these two rifles, the one the defendant allegedly used to commit the murder and the one known to be legitimately owned by him?"

The gun specialist spent a few minutes examining the two rifles carefully with a magnifying glass.

"Please be careful not to touch the rifles if at all possible," Kane requested.

Kane asked Swartz about his conclusions when he finished the examination.

Swartz sat back down on the witness stand and said, "Based on minute scratches on both the trigger guards and the triggers, I'd say that somebody swapped out the trigger guards on these two rifles."

"What do you mean by 'minute scratches'?" Kane asked.

Swartz said, "The murder weapon doesn't have any scratches to speak of. It clearly hasn't been used much. Somebody probably fired it a handful of times to align the sights and then to commit the murder. But the defendant's rifle has been used a lot. When I compared the minute scratches on its trigger with the scratches on the trigger guard of the murder weapon, they were a match."

Kane contemplated Swartz' statement for a moment. "So, in your professional opinion, someone removed the trigger guards from both of these guns and swapped them out?"

"Yes, sir."

Bowling had nothing to ask Swartz and declined the invitation with a perplexed look on his face.

Kane was able to retrieve the information he needed from Swartz. He called the forensics expert back to the stand. He began by asking,

"We've learned that a single fingerprint was found on the trigger guard of the murder weapon just in front of the trigger. Somebody wiped the rest of the gun clean. An expert confirmed that the fingerprint belongs to the defendant. I understand the art of fingerprinting is a simple one?"

"Certainly. Most officers are trained in the procedure."

"Could it be done here and now? The fingerprint found on the trigger guard of the murder weapon was the only fingerprint found on the entire rifle.

Would it be possible to fingerprint the other rifle, the one legitimately known to be owned by the defendant?"

The witness looked a little confused, "Why yes. I suppose so. You mean right now? We'd need a kit. We might find one in one of the police cruisers outside in the parking lot. I'd say the sheriff's cruiser would have one for sure."

"Objection, Your Honor," Bowling barked, "This is highly unusual. Now we're going to go out into the parking lot on a wild-goose chase for fingerprinting kits?"

"Overruled," Judge Newman said as he directed Bowling's attention to the large shower stall he'd drug into the courtroom.

The judge was intrigued about where Kane was going with his questions. He added, "Someone has already taken a woman's life from her. Now a young man's life is on the line. I think it behooves us to do whatever it takes to test the accusation against the defendant. It'd be just as wrong for us to condemn an innocent man for this crime as it was for the murderer to take his victim's life.

"Sheriff Brown," the judge continued, "do you have the necessary tools in your cruiser to fingerprint the defendant's gun?"

"Yes, sir," the sheriff said. He got up and went to fetch the kit.

Sheriff Brown returned to the courtroom with the fingerprinting kit. He handed it to Kane who then passed it along to the forensics expert. The expert carefully went through the procedure of fingerprinting Jeremy's sniper rifle. He returned to the witness stand when he finished.

"Now that you've fingerprinted the defendant's rifle, what are your conclusions?" Kane asked.

"I was able to see several fingerprints all over the rifle. Those fingerprints match up with the defendant's as would be expected."

"You fingerprinted the entire gun? You found prints everywhere on the gun?"

"That's correct."

"Did you find any prints on the trigger?"

"I did."

"And what about the trigger guard? Did you find any prints there?"

"No, sir."

"What was that? You say there were no prints on the trigger guard?"

"None."

"Nowhere on the trigger guard?"

"No, sir. It looks like somebody wiped it clean."

"Isn't it strange that the defendant's prints are all over his rifle, including the trigger, yet there's not a single smudge on the entirety of the trigger guard?"

"Objection, Your Honor," Bowling said. "Can we stick to facts rather than trying to determine what is or is not strange?"

"I'll determine what the facts are or are not in this courtroom, Mr. Bowling," the judge said. "Nevertheless, I'm going to sustain the objection."

"Thank you, Your Honor," Kane said. "I have nothing else for this witness."

The judge sustained Bowling's objection, but Kane knew the judge realized the significance of what the forensics expert discovered when he fingerprinted Jeremy's rifle. It was obvious that someone had swapped out the trigger guards between those guns. Kane was certain that the judge was asking himself, "Why would Jeremy do such a thing if he committed the murder?"

"Just wait till you see what's next," Kane thought to himself.

TWENTY-EIGHT

THE MID-AFTERNOON WEATHER was beautiful outside the courthouse. It brought the kind of peace only a late spring day in Tennessee could bring. The trees were lush in rich green colors. Their leaves danced playfully in the light breeze. Spring flowers were in full bloom, and their sweet scent filled the air. Cars scarcely drove by. A handful of people sat on benches around the property. Some read for pleasure. Others ate a late lunch.

Things were much different inside the courthouse. Jeremy was scared, but his face was beginning to show some hope. His mom sat a few seats back and looked weak and frightened. She was concerned about the now uncertain future of her only child. Bowling was shuffling papers at his table and trying to figure out what Kane had up his sleeve.

Kane walked over to the defense table to retrieve

the small Ziploc bag Earl brought him when the large entrance doors in the back of the courtroom opened. An officer escorted an older woman through the doors and to a seat. She was rambling irritably about being drug out of her garden and down to the courthouse. Earl looked around and recognized her. It was Mrs. Foster, the woman who sold him the worthless tractor. He'd forgotten all about it and hadn't sent anyone by to get the tractor.

The doors opened again, and another officer entered with an old man by his side. Unlike Mrs. Foster, the old man was quiet and relaxed and appeared to be happy to be there. It was Quinton Gray—the ninety-five-year-old man who lived directly behind the field where the murderer fired the deadly shot. Kane texted Frank during the ride back from Smyrna and asked him to arrange for a couple of officers to go by and see if they could persuade Mr. Gray and Mrs. Foster to come down to the courthouse and give testimony about what they heard on the morning of the murder. Bowling left nothing to chance. He unloaded all of his most significant evidence to get Jeremy's case sent to the Grand Jury. Kane wasn't going to leave anything to chance when it came to unraveling every detail of Bowling's evidence.

Kane entered the contents of the Ziploc bag into evidence. Then he handed it to the forensics expert who was still on the witness stand—a single bullet.

"Do you recognize this bullet?" Kane asked.

"It appears to be the same as the bullet found in the body of the victim."

"The bullet that killed Linda Richards is lying on

the evidence table," Kane said. "You've determined it was fired from the rifle that's been identified as the murder weapon. Can you also determine if the same rifle fired this bullet?"

Bowling sprang up in his seat. "What's he doing?" he said to himself. "Another bullet? Where did that come from? Only one shot was fired that morning." He watched anxiously as the forensic expert went over to the table to examine the new bullet. The expert returned to the stand when he finished the examination.

"What did you discover?" Kane asked.

"There's no doubt about it. The same rifle fired both of those bullets," the witness said as he handed the bullet back to Kane.

"Objection, Your Honor," Bowling said rather abruptly. "What's the point of all of this? Another bullet? Fired from the same rifle that killed Linda Richards? Big deal! What does it prove? Mr. Swartz already testified that the killer probably fired the rifle a handful of times to set the sights. This new bullet could be one of those bullets. And how could we know if it was even fired on the same morning the murder occurred? And what difference would it make anyway?"

The judge looked at Kane with a questioning expression on his face. Kane shrugged his shoulders and asked the forensic expert, "Is there any way to determine if this bullet was fired on the morning of the murder?"

"As a matter of fact, there may be," the witness said.

Both Kane and Bowling looked at the witness

dumbfounded.

"Really?" Kane thought. He caught himself before he said it out loud. "Maybe this will be easier than I thought." Out loud he said, "Can you explain what you mean?"

"Well, a year or so ago, I was reading an old article in The American Journal of Police Science. The article dealt with the effect glass has on a bullet when it passes through it. One section of the article dealt with the deformation that can occur in a bullet when it passes through glass."

"Oh?" Kane said. "Please continue."

The witness said, "I found the article and read it again when this case with Linda Richards came up because it involved a bullet that had passed through glass. Not only does the article describe the deformation that can occur in the bullet, but it also refers to some tests that were made by shooting bullets through glass panels and into some bags of sawdust. They dug the bullets out of the sawdust and found finely-powdered glass embedded in the nose and cannelures of the bullets. I decided to examine the bullet that killed Linda Richards. Surprisingly, there was no powdered glass to be found. That was odd because the bullet passed through not one but two panels of glass. It was also interesting that none of the deformation described in the article was present in the bullet."

"This is unbelievable," Kane thought to himself. "It supports the conclusion I came to this morning when I remembered what was troubling me about the shower stall!"

Everything made sense to Kane! A thought

suddenly occurred to him. He asked the witness, "What about the second bullet, the one I entered into evidence a few moments ago. Did you test it for any of these signs when you examined it?"

"I did."

"What did you find?"

"Curiously enough, that bullet possesses all the characteristics the article mentioned. Not only is there finely-powdered glass in the nose and cannelure of the bullet, but there's some on the outside of the jacket too. The deformation is there too. If I hadn't dug the first bullet out of the victim myself, I'd think it was this second bullet that killed Linda Richards."

"Your Honor, please." Bowling protested. "None of this makes any sense."

"Your Honor," Kane said, "I believe I can show the significance of this new information if you'll bear with me."

"Very well. Overruled," Judge Newman said. "I'll hear the rest of it, Mr. Kane, but the afternoon is wearing on. I advise you to make it quick."

"Yes, Your Honor, thank you. I'd like to call Sheriff Gary Brown to the stand."

"Sheriff Brown," Kane said, "tell us about this second bullet we've been discussing. Where was it found?"

"Yes, sir. It was found in the field on the south side of the Richards' house about thirty yards out just in line with where the shower stall was sitting on the deck."

"You mean the *north* side?" Kane asked. He wanted to emphasize the significance of what the sheriff said.

"No, sir. I mean on the *south* side."

Kane said, "But that's the side from which the shot came. This bullet should've been in the field on the north side of the Richards' house if it was fired from the south side and passed through that shower stall."

The sheriff shrugged, "I agree, but it is what it is."

"You found this bullet on the south side of the house, and the bullet clearly passed through the shower stall. The only possible conclusion is that this bullet must've been fired from the other side of the Richards' house, the north side, and *not* from the south side."

The sheriff looked at Kane for a moment, "Is that a question?" he asked.

Kane shrugged, "Sure."

"Well, then, yes. It seems clear that this bullet was fired from the field that lies to the north of the Richards' house rather than from the field that lies to the south toward the Hensley's house where the defendant was staying."

"Who found the bullet?" Kane asked.

"I found it earlier this afternoon along with my deputies," the sheriff said.

"Did you find any other bullets?"

"No, and we scanned the entire area thoroughly."

"Thank you, Sheriff. I have no further questions, Your Honor."

"Mr. Bowling?" The Judge asked.

Bowling scratched his head and said reluctantly, "I have nothing to add, Your Honor."

With the groundwork laid, Kane was ready to call Jim Tenry back to the stand. He wanted to make sure he'd introduced everything else before he brought out the salient details of Jim Tenry's testimony because Tenry's testimony wouldn't just take the limelight off of Jeremy, it would implicate someone else specifically as the murderer. Kane didn't want to make that implication unless there was some substantial evidence already in place.

Tenry took the stand, and Kane said, "Mr. Tenry, you told us earlier that Don Richards began visiting the main office of SWAG about two weeks ago. He explained that he wanted to take a more personal interest in the businesses his investment group owns. Is that correct?"

"Yes, sir."

"Was he interested in anything specific?"

"He wanted to learn the hands-on stuff. He was particularly interested in learning about the shower stalls. He said that, since he owned one, maybe he should learn how to repair it in case it ever got damaged."

Kane's eyebrows lifted knowingly. The judge perked up. Bowling shifted nervously in his seat. Bowling surmised that there must be a connection between what Tenry just said and the information about the second bullet. But he couldn't make out what the connection could be.

Kane paced in thought for a few moments. He was trying to decide exactly how to go about extracting the information he wanted Tenry to reveal. He finally stopped pacing and asked,

"What exactly did Mr. Richards want to know

about the stalls?"

"Well, there's not really much to learn," Tenry said. "I mostly spent time teaching him how to change out the glass panels in case they were damaged."

"You taught him yourself? You didn't have one of your employees teach him?"

"Yes, sir. I taught him myself."

"These glass panels," Kane said. "About how long would it take to change out, say, two of them?"

"Well, if a professional did the work, it'd probably take about an hour and a half to do the job properly."

"An hour and a half? But wouldn't it be as simple as removing the old panels and sliding in the new ones?"

"Well, he'd need to install new rubber seals and so forth to prevent leaks. That takes a bit more time."

"Would Don Richards be capable of doing the job properly in about an hour and a half?"

"Yes, as I said, I taught him myself. He's spent a lot of time practicing too. I'd say he could do it in an hour and a half. No more than two hours anyway."

Kane asked, "What if someone didn't care about leaks? What if they simply replaced the panels and stuck the old seals back in?"

"I wouldn't recommend it, but that'd be a simple matter. Anybody who was familiar with the process could do it in fifteen minutes or less."

"What if somebody wanted to reverse the existing panels to make them face the other way without changing the seals? Would that also take fifteen minutes or less?"

Bowling's eyes widened. What Kane was driving at finally hit him. In fact, everything hit him. He was beginning to see what Kane saw in his mind earlier that morning. He was making the connections. He stood up and tried to object again. The judge shot him down. The judge was connecting the dots too. He wanted to hear more.

"Yes. I suppose so," Tenry answered.

Kane asked, "Could somebody detect if the panels had been reversed by simply looking at the stall?"

Tenry said, "They'd have to know what they were looking for and they'd have to be intentionally looking for it. It'd certainly be detected the next time somebody used the stall. It'd leak something furious!"

Kane turned and paced slowly toward the audience and raised his voice slightly so everyone could hear him, "If I understand you correctly, somebody could reverse those panels in less than fifteen minutes if they didn't replace the seals, and no one would know they did it unless they took a shower in the stall?"

"Without a thorough examination from someone who knew about shower stalls, that's correct."

"Would you say that Don Richards has the skill to reverse those panels in fifteen minutes or less?"

"No doubt about it," Tenry said.

Don Richards' face was expressionless. He sat quietly and listened with interest.

"Mr. Tenry," Kane said, "if you were to inspect

this shower stall, would you be able to determine if somebody has reversed the front and back panels?"

"Absolutely," Tenry said.

Tenry got up and walked toward the stall. He began by inspecting the seals around the back panel. He looked at them closely. Then he simply pulled on one of the rubber strips from the top. The entire vertical strip fell right off. Someone had clearly stuck it into place quickly. He did the same thing with the other vertical strip and the top and bottom horizontal strips. Then he simply pulled the panel out.

There was a hushed gasp from the audience. Everyone could see that someone had quickly removed the panel, turned it around, and then put it back in with the old rubber stripping.

Kane said, "Thank you, Mr. Tenry. I believe that's all I'll need from you."

Bowling was stunned by what he saw. He couldn't think of any questions to ask Jim Tenry.

Kane called Larry Clemmons back to the stand. Clemmons was one of the lead detectives who investigated the crime scene. Kane could've called the sheriff back up to get what he was after next, but he wanted to involve as many of Bowling's witnesses as he could. It would add force to his evidence.

Clemmons had already put two and two together from everything he'd just seen and heard. He was trying to rearrange all the particulars of the crime scene in his mind. Everything was backward from what they'd all thought from the beginning.

Kane asked Clemmons, "Mr. Clemmons, just as

a reminder, you were a lead detective on Linda Richards' crime scene from the beginning?"

"Yes, sir."

"And you investigated every aspect of the crime scene thoroughly?"

"Absolutely!" Clemmons was almost offended at the question.

"And you paid close attention to the shower stall?"

"I certainly did."

Kane handed Clemmons a couple of pictures of the stall that included the portion of the deck just around it, "Tell me, Mr. Clemmons, do you see any water or dampness at all on the deck that immediately surrounds the shower stall?"

"No, sir. And I remember that in particular. The portion of the deck around the stall wasn't wet at all."

Kane said, "But based on everything we've just heard and seen from Jim Tenry, if somebody reversed those panels without replacing the rubber stripping, that stall would've leaked 'something furious,' as he put it. But the deck around the stall was bone dry. What would you deduce from this as a highly skilled detective?"

"Objection," Bowling spat out loudly. He hoped his insistence would add force to his plea for an objection. "That calls for supposition."

"Overruled!" the judge snapped back.

"Mr. Bowling," the judge continued, "I'm pretty sure everyone present has already deduced the answer to Mr. Kane's question by now. Somebody may as well say it out loud."

The judge turned to Clemmons, “Please answer the question, detective.”

Clemmons said, “From everything I’ve just heard, along with the fact that the deck was dry, it’s clear that somebody reversed those two shower stall panels *after* Linda Richards was shot and not before. They would’ve had to practically step over the body to do so,” he added with a grimace on his face. “And then, when you factor in the results of the examination of the second bullet the sheriff found on the south side of the Richards’ house, it seems to me that Linda Richards wasn’t shot from the south side of the house at all. Somebody shot her from the field on the other side of the house, the north side.”

The audience began to murmur. The judge tapped his gavel lightly to call everyone back to order. They’d made a lot of connections in light of all the new evidence, but most of them hadn’t carried the conclusion quite that far yet. But they saw it when Clemmons made his statement, and Kane was extremely satisfied with the effect.

“I have no further questions for this witness, Your Honor,” Kane said.

Bowling was anxious to quit warming the bench. He sprang from his feet when the judge asked if he wanted to question the witness.

Bowling said to the witness, “Detective Clemmons, I want to remind all of us that this hearing is about the charges the state has brought against the defendant, Jeremy Scott. Let’s suppose the deductions you just offered are correct. How would they negate the state’s charges? Mr. Scott could've just as easily shot Linda Richards from the north side of the house as he could've from the south side."

"Perhaps," Clemmons said, looking doubtful. He didn't want to cross the popular Assistant DA.

"Thank you, detective." Bowling walked back to his table with a bit of a strut in his gait. "No further questions, Your Honor."

Kane called the sheriff back to the stand. He said,

"Sheriff Brown, it's been conclusively shown that the time of death was five minutes after seven last Tuesday morning. Linda Richards died almost instantly after somebody shot her directly in the heart. There's no doubt about it in light of the evidence. So the killer fired the deadly shot at five minutes after seven. I can personally vouch for Jeremy Scott's whereabouts at seven thirty-five that same morning. He was in my office. That's about a fifteen-minute drive from the Hensley's house. He would've had to leave the Hensley's house at twenty minutes after seven. That's just fifteen minutes after Linda Richards was shot. Based on your investigation, remind us of everything the defendant would've had to accomplish during that fifteen minutes. Please base your answer on the scenario that he fired the shot from the south side of the Richards' house, the side near the Hensley's house where he was staying."

"Certainly," the sheriff said with an intense, thoughtful expression. "First, he would've had to run one hundred and thirty-seven yards back to the Hensley's house from the patch of trees in the field.

Then he would've had to crawl under the Hensley's house, inch his way to the front side of the house, and then bury the gun a foot deep. Then he would've had to enter the house, change his shoes, and probably his clothes, and then walk out to his car."

"Is it possible to accomplish all of that in the fifteen minutes?" Kane asked.

"He could just make it if he dug the hole under the house at a previous time," the sheriff said.

"Have you tested this?" Kane asked.

"Yes, I had one of my officers go through the motions. It's very close, but it's possible."

"Did the investigators find the dirty clothes he wore when he did the shooting?"

"No, but he could've taken those with him and disposed of them in any number of ways."

"Now," Kane said, "In light of the new evidence, it seems clear that the shooting was done from the *north* side of the Richards' house rather than from the *south* side. We've also established that somebody reversed the two panels on the shower stall presumably to give the impression that the shot came from the south side of the house. And that's the conclusion everyone came to initially. The shooter reversed the panels so the bullet holes would be on the opposite sides of the panels from where they actually entered the stall. Given this scenario, what would your answer be to my previous question?"

"In that scenario, you'd have to add another one hundred and sixty yards to the distance he'd need to travel on foot back to the Hensley's house. You'd also have to add the time it would take to reverse the glass panels in the shower stall. Either one of these additions by itself would make it humanly impossible for the defendant to accomplish all the things I listed within the fifteen minutes he had available to him."

That was the answer that ended it all. If it was true that the deadly shot came from the field on the north side of the house instead of from the field on the south side of the house, Jeremy couldn't have murdered Linda Richards.

Kane was certain that the judge agreed with the second scenario—that the bullet came from the north side of the house. And with the sheriff's testimony, the judge would have no choice but to dismiss the case and grant Jeremy his freedom.

If the judge still had doubts, Kane would call Mrs. Foster and Quinton Gray to the stand. Mrs. Foster's house sat close to the field on the north side of the Richards' house, and she was certain she heard two shots. But Mr. Gray's house was directly behind the field that lay between the Richards' house and the Hensley's house. And he didn't hear *any* shots that morning. Their combined testimony would strengthen the compelling evidence they'd already presented and leave no doubt that the killer shot Linda Richards from the opposite field than was originally thought. The crowd in the courtroom became excitedly loud again while Kane ran those thoughts through his head.

It took the judge a few moments to get everyone in the courtroom calmed down. Then he spoke with clarity and authority. His words were few and to the point. "In light of the evidence presented here today, I find that this case should *not* be bound over to the Grand Jury. I'm dismissing this case with the state's sincere apologies to Jeremy Scott and his family. Mr. Scott, you are free to go."

Leann jumped to her feet with excitement. Jeremy sat stunned and wondered if it was real. His mother rushed across the courtroom to his side. They embraced.

The DA had the right to bring the same charges against Jeremy at a later date since there wasn't a trial. But the evidence Kane presented at the hearing gave the DA a much better suspect to investigate.

Kane remained calm and emotionless when he heard the judge's ruling. Earl was smiling and shaking hands with Sheriff Brown. Mrs. Foster was whining about losing quality time in her garden for nothing. Quinton Gray was inviting a couple of officers over for some iced tea, and Assistant DA Bowling sat quietly at his table with a dumfounded, bewildered, and defeated expression on his face.

TWENTY-NINE

KANE, LEANN, AND EARL sat in Kane's office and discussed the case later that evening. Jeremy, his mom, and Roger drove back to the Scott's house on Heavenly Way after everyone dispersed from the courthouse. Jeremy and Roger went to the Hensley's house to pack up Jeremy's belongings—those the police hadn't confiscated. They planned to stay with Jeremy's mom. They didn't want to stay at the Hensley's house after everything that had happened, and Mrs. Scott didn't want to be alone.

Kane sipped his coffee from his dark burgundy cup while Leann nursed a bottle of spring water.

"What made you see it?" Leann asked Kane. "How'd you finally figure it out?"

"Mildew," Kane said.

"Mildew?" Earl said.

"Yes, mildew. That's what I kept trying to remember. At the crime scene, Leann said she could never have an outdoor shower stall because mildew builds up on it too quickly. Then we discussed the Richards' glass shower stall. We noticed a slight haze of mildew on the panels. I could barely see it. That's what occurred to me when I was looking at the stall in the courtroom. The sunlight was shining on the panels in such a way that I could see that haze of mildew. The mildew was on the inside of the side panels, but it was on the outside of the front and back panels—the ones the bullet passed through. That didn't make any sense. It occurred to me that someone must've reversed the panels the bullet passed through."

Kane's phone rang. He put it to his ear and said, "Hello Frank."

Leann and Earl went out into the front office while Kane spoke to Frank. She'd asked Earl a technical question about computers earlier. He was showing her something on the computer at the secretary's desk.

"Don Richards was pretty clever in how he planned it all out," Leann said. "He didn't really make many mistakes when you think about it."

"Yes," Earl said, "but it was that one big mistake he made that got him caught. If he hadn't made that mistake, he might've gotten away with murdering his wife and practically taking Jeremy's life away from him by framing him for the murder."

"What big mistake was that?" Leann asked.

"With that bogus business card along with the bogus abduction letter, he sent Jeremy right into the office of Tyler Kane."

They returned to Kane's office a few minutes later. Kane had just finished talking to Frank.

"What did Frank know?" Earl asked.

Kane said, "The DA sent a technical expert out to the Richards' house to search through his computer because of the evidence I brought out during the hearing. I also mentioned a few things to Bowling after the hearing was over. They found a deleted file that turned out to be those bogus 'Tyler Kane' business cards. That was all they needed to arrest Don Richards on suspicion of murder. When they went to arrest him, he broke down and confessed everything in detail."

"Why did he do it?" Leann asked. "He and his wife were very happy and still very much in love from everything we heard."

"I'm not sure if we ever truly know anyone, Leann," Kane said. "But Don Richards' reason for murdering his wife came right down to the old motive of insurance money."

"Insurance money?" Leann exclaimed.

"Yes, he had a substantial debt from his gambling tryst out in Vegas if you'll remember. His losses were likely more significant than we thought. The insurance money from his wife's death would've covered all those losses and kept him afloat financially."

"What about Johnny Ray?" Earl asked. "Why did Don Richards mimic Johnny Ray's speech when he bought that M107 rifle from Rabbit's friend?"

"Simple," Kane said. "He originally planned to frame Johnny Ray for the murder. Then he figured it'd be easier to frame Jeremy when he learned he'd be staying at the Hensley's house for a couple of weeks. He had something to use as a motive regardless of which one he framed.

"The irony is that when he changed plans at the last minute it helped him in a way he couldn't have anticipated. It threw a curveball in our direction. It sent us off on a wild goose chase to investigate Johnny Ray and wasted a lot of the precious little time we had. That almost got Jeremy sent to the Grand Jury. It was just pure luck that I noticed that mildew this morning. Jeremy would still be sitting behind bars down at the county jail if Leann hadn't brought up that discussion about mildew in the first place."

Leann's face lit up. The case was over, and she hoped she and Kane would soon discuss whether or not she'd be his assistant on a full-time basis.

"What made you think about the trigger guards? How'd you know somebody swapped them out between the two rifles?" Leann asked.

"I'll have to give Earl credit for that one. He insists on making detailed notes of his interviews. He even writes down things that seem insignificant. Truth be told, I got lucky. Earl told me about Jeremy's M107 rifle because he saw it at the Scott's house when he interviewed Jeremy's mother. But he mentioned in his notes that Don Richards came over to build a ramp off their foyer while Mrs. Scott was visiting her doctors. That would've given Don an opportunity to swap out the trigger guards between the two rifles. It doesn't take long to do if the person knows what he's doing. And we all know that Don Richards' is knowledgeable and skilled when it comes to sniper rifles."

"How'd Don Richards get into the Hensley's

house to grab Jeremy's shoes?" Leann asked.

"Jeremy's mother told Earl that all three of those families on Heavenly Way are very close. They've got keys to each other's houses in case of emergencies and such."

"I'm still not sure I understand exactly how he did it. Why'd he need to fire two shots?" Leann asked.

"Simple," Kane said. "He fired the shots one right after the other. Remember, he made the shot from the north side of the house instead of the south side. But he wanted to make it look like he shot her from the south side. He intentionally fired the first shot right past his wife and through the panels of the shower stall. Then he fired the second shot into her back."

"So the bullet that killed Mrs. Richards hit her directly. It didn't pass through the shower stall."

"Exactly. That's why the forensics expert didn't find any glass powder on or in the bullet that killed her. If Don had fired from the north side of the house, the shower stall would've been *behind* his wife rather than *between* him and her. He had a direct shot. He fired the first shot through the glass panels so he could reverse the panels and make it look like somebody shot her from south side of the house from the field that lies between their house and the Hensley's. That would make it easier to frame Jeremy because he was staying at the Hensley's house."

Leann said, "Wow! That took some sharp shooting."

"Don Richards is a sharpshooter. Remember,

he's a trained sniper."

"Of course," Leann said.

Kane continued, "Don went to the Hensley's house right after his wife left for her morning walk and before Jeremy arrived there from work. He planted the bogus abduction note and set the alarm on the alarm clock. Then he got Jeremy's shoes and probably put them on when he got back to where he planned to do the shooting. He had to move fast after he made the shots. He reversed the glass panels which probably took about fifteen minutes. He finished right about the time Jeremy left to go to my office. With Jeremy gone, he went to the patch of trees between his house and the Hensley's house to make some footprints around the trees, scuff up some bark, and plant the ten-foot-long strap in the tree. Then he went to the Hensley's house to bury the gun under the house and return Jeremy's shoes."

"That was a tight time frame. Like I told Earl earlier, he certainly planned everything out well," Leann said.

Kane sipped his coffee, "Yes. He did."

Earl said in a casual tone, "Well, I've got to get home to the family, Cuz. It's been fun." He walked toward the door as if figuring out the crime was just a stroll in the park. "Give me a call when the next big case comes up."

"Thank you, Earl," Kane said. "Call me in the morning. I'll buy you lunch."

"Chinese buffet?" Earl said.

"Anything you want," Kane said. "See you tomorrow."

"Well, you know?" Leann began after Earl was

gone. “I’m exhausted from all of this, you know? I think I’m going to be heading out too, you know? See you in the morning, Mr. Kane, you know?”

Kane looked up at Leann as she stood at the door with a grin on her face. One corner of his mouth curled up slightly, and he said with a hint of a sparkle in his dark hazel eyes, “’kay.”

-The End

AUTHOR'S NOTES

Dear Reader. I humbly thank you for reading my little story. I hope you enjoyed it. If so, please consider writing a review on Amazon. Also, my next Tyler Kane adventure, "The BC Killer." Can be found on Amazon as well.

In real life, there may be a Gray Road and a Heavenly Way; I haven't checked. I just made mine up. Their names and any other similarities to actual streets are entirely coincidental.

All of the businesses in this book are products of my imagination. Devilish Dunkers, RoundFun, Inc., Carla's Country Catheads, IIC (Innovative Inventors Club), SWAG, and PharmBright were all created by me. Any resemblance to actual businesses or their names is entirely coincidental.

If anything I have imagined in this novel bears any resemblance to actual people, whether living or dead, events, locations, et.al, it is wholly by coincidence.

My story sometimes sheds official servants in a bad light. That's fiction! In real life, I have the utmost respect for those who work in criminal law. They work long, difficult hours and often at great personal sacrifice in order to keep me and my family safe. I am thankful for their dedication. I encourage everyone to give them their full respect, support, encouragement, and cooperation.

I am not wholly ignorant of the law or its workings. Nevertheless, I have taken some liberties in order to make my story work. If you need to learn about actual law, I highly recommend consulting an actual lawyer or law books. If you want to relax and enjoy a fictional story, please continue to read my books.

Thank you so much! I appreciate you!

-Michael Pickford

Made in the USA
Middletown, DE
06 April 2021

37048842R00149